TERRIBLE FRIEND

TERRIBLE FRIEND

CHRISTY MANN

Cover Design by Henry Dalton

Twisted Souls Press

This is a work of fiction. All characters and events portrayed in this book are either products of the author's imagination or are used fictionally.
Publisher
Twisted Souls Press LLC
www.twistedsoulspress.com
For rights, bulk publishing, and other publication information or to report errors, email a letter to:
Twisted Souls Press LLC
twistedsoulspress@gmail.com
Twisted Souls Press Logo image
Adam Mitchell 2019

Cover Design by Henry Dalton

CONTENTS

Terrible Terrible Friend

I see your weakness
You make me smile
With lies that are seamless
Hiding what I've known all the while
If I let you in the know
You'd be so rightfully scared
What I'll never show
Is just what you've thought and feared
I am your terrible terrible friend
Into your heart I can easily see
Yet I love you completely without end
Even though you do not really know me
Before you all this time
I stood patient and smiled
Written in poetic rhyme
Now I tell you simple Child
I am your terrible terrible friend
You I would never think to betray
And to hell I gladly would send
Every evil thinking to cross your way
I am far from good
I am plainly no saint
But by you I've stood

Suffering quietly without complaint
I am your terrible terrible friend
With pleasure I'd let you see
I am your terrible terrible friend
More and more you would love me
In my love I am not wrong
You are worth it to me
Horrible true and strong
But you don't really know me
About me It is ok
Go on in your life
Believe what they say
I would not bring you strife
Just feel it knowing inside
When you look blindly my way
I'd destroy the helpless world with pride
For you alone making your way
I am your terrible terrible friend
Proverbial menace more than man
I wallow happily in miserable sin
My redemption is that I'll save you if I can
I'd swim through the pits of hell
Killing demon and man
Become an empty shell
Jump into the fires from the pan
I'd watch the innocent die

Rape the knowledge from the gods
Tell every known lie
Fight against any odds
I am your terrible terrible friend
And to heaven you'll go
Riding on my back without sin
Even the Devil will know
On your head not to touch
So much as a hair
I am your crutch
I make this game fair
Never will you know me
For the terror that I am
I do not hide it see
You just don't understand
I am your terrible terrible friend
Golden gods of heaven will bow
To my will in the end
I will save you for good and for now
I am your terrible terrible friend
It is my job to save
All that they would condemn
Try to be brave
I am your terrible terrible friend
Your punishments I'd take
Hell is mine and to them I lend

Those who's love is fake
I am your terrible terrible friend
Believe what you will
I need no faith to send
My challenge and wish ill
On all those who judged
You and all who condemn
I will not be budged
I am your terrible terrible friend

~Christopher
Spitler*

CHAPTER 1

Albert sat up. He was on the beach, the cool breeze off the waves blew into his face. Filling his nostrils with the scents of salt and seaweed. He looked out across the water, reveling in the momentary silence and calm inside his head. He knew it would be short lived, but he was determined to enjoy it for as long as he could. He recalled the events of the night before and stretched and cursed under his breath.

He looked around, taking in the emptiness and serenity of the public beach. The deep purple of the starless sky above him and the lights of the hotels on around him told him it was very early. He had arrived her just a few hours ago and was pondering why he was awake so early in a place that he could usually sleep so soundly.

This was the only place in the last 38 years that would silence the cacophony of voices in his head and he could rest peacefully. Something about the vast number of stars above him and the waves crashing in the darkness would lull them to a dull roar, and he could sleep. He was rarely awake before 9am on this beach. Usually aroused by an aggressively spiked beach ball rolling gently into his shoulder or poked at with a stick by some youngsters checking to see if they had indeed found a large dead and bloated body on the beach, this morning, there were neither. Just him, the sky, and the waves spilling gently onto the shore 10 feet from his toes.

The first voices started mumbling in his head. He sighed. The silence never lasted long once his eyes were open. He started every morning with a quick prayer that one day he wouldn't be bothered by them anymore. To date, no satisfactory answer had come.

<Why are we awake so early Al> The loudest voice rang through his head.

Albert ignored it. It was more of a rhetorical question anyway. No answer would suffice, and Albert just wasn't ready to deal with the barrage of questions that Jax would inundate him with this early in the day.

He took a deep breath, crossed his fingers behind his head, laid back in the sand, and exhaled slowly as the chorus of voices sang out inside his headspace.

This was the chaos, the resonance of what seemed like a thousand voices, all speaking at the same time, but never saying anything he could make out.

Whispers with lingering esses, moans and groans, bickering and cackling laughter would ring in the back of his head. He could force himself to ignore that part.

Jax, however, would not, be ignored. <Al! Why are we up so early?>

Albert, plagued by the question himself, sat up and took another look around. There were no people about, no sea birds cackling above him, so he really didn't have an answer. He shifted his weight and laid back. He found the culprit.

A sharp point was jabbing him in the side. He reached

under himself and pulled out a chunk of metal. He held his hand out in front of him as he sat up and examined the object in his hand.

A heavy silver chain spilled from his hand and dangled. Sparkling gently as it swung side to side. In the palm of his hand was a large claw-like hand that clung with all its might to a large dark green stone. He examined it gently. The chain looked old and like it had been both pounded with a hammer and chiseled out of a block of silver. The hand that held the stone looked like it had been poured and then scraped with a pick to create the intricate details of 3 sharp talons. "It might have been this?" He listened for a response from Jax.

There wasn't one. He noticed a strange buzzing sensation in his head. Like clippers were being run up the back of his scalp, but on the inside. The racket that had been blaring just a moment ago was hushed. He turned his hand over and let the necklace slip back onto the sand.

The moment the necklace left Albert's hand, the buzzing stopped, a symphony of voices rose up again and Jax bellowed. <What the hell was that!?> Albert didn't respond. <Al!!! What was that?> The voice boomed.

Jax commanded an answer that shook Albert out of his confused state. He had never heard Jax speak like that before. He was always a pompous ass, pushy and demanding, but this was different. It was base like he had never heard before and it shook him violently for just a moment.

Albert finally answered. "It's a necklace. An old, ugly one."

<A necklace?> Jax voice was normal again.

"Yes, a necklace. What's your problem?"

<Of course, you just shock the ever-loving shit out of me, and you want to know what my problem is?>

"Shock the...what are you talking about?" Albert reached for the necklace again.

<DO NOT!!!> The booming voice returned.

Albert sat back and stared at the necklace. Wide eyed and perplexed, he froze as Jax and the other voices flew into a full-blown rage inside his head.

The multitude of voices wailed and screamed. Jax mumbled things in a language Albert had never heard before. He cupped his hands over his ears, trying to shut out the noise within.

Slowly, Albert reached for the chain once more. The chortling continued. He gripped the chain tightly and lifted it up in front of him. The chaos in his head steadily increased to a crescendo he could physically feel. He grabbed the charm with his other hand and there was the slightest hint of a gasp and then silence.

The buzzing in the back of his skull returned and the silence continued. He released the charm. The sound of an exhale and then the chaos of wailing and cursing and foreign languages started again.

Albert wrapped his hand around the charm once more before Jax could utter more than a scream.

He repeated the process several times, grasping different parts of the charm, trying to wrap his mind around what was happening. When he felt he could garner no more information from the process, he set the necklace back down on the sand.

Jax abruptly and crudely cursed Albert. <You degenerate asshole. If you touch it again, I will make your head explode!>

Albert chuckled. Other than the buzzing feeling and the silence, he felt no ill effects. Jax and the rest being the result of a chemical imbalance, as he had been told when he was young, the heated threat was anything but threatening. "Why not? I enjoy the silence."

<We need to leave it. Get away from it. Let's go!>

"Leave it? Why would we do that? It belongs to somebody and I'm sure they would like it back."

<Absolutely not! Bury it back in the sand and walk away! Do it! Do it now!>

"No stupid. We return lost things. We don't leave them where we found them. What is wrong with you?"

Jax hesitated and then growled. <Nothing is wrong with me. Just put that thing back and let's get out of here.>

"I will not." Albert picked up the chain. "You always demand that we return something we have found. You are not telling me something for some reason and we will sit here, staring at this ugly jewelry, until you either tell me what it is, or who it belongs to so we can return it!!"

Jax growled again. <This is not a game Albert. Nothing good will come of this. Bury it and walk away.>

"Thirty years Jax. Thirty damn years and I don't care if it was a copper penny that was lost. If we found it, we returned it. If it was lost, we found it. This is what we do. So, what the hell is wrong with you?"

Albert didn't normally argue with Jax about things. He thought it stupid to argue with a figment of his imagination, so he just did what he felt he should do. This always, somehow miraculously, resulted in the item being returned to its rightful owner. This time though, his figment was being a little too coy. Something was up. So, he sat with his arms crossed. Determined not to move until he got his answer.

When they had sat there for an hour, Albert deliberately toying with Jax by moving his hand closer and then away from the necklace, Jax relented. <FINE! We need to return it. NOW!!!>

"Ok, return it to who?"

<I don't know who she is, but she wants it back very badly.>

"Who is she?"

<I don't know, I can't see her.>

"Then how do you know it's a she?" Albert was finding joy in pulling Jax's strings for a change. He was often giving Jax a hard time about his self-proclaimed psychic abilities. Albert didn't believe in those kinds of things, but Jax did seem to have a knack for finding things. He thought maybe a voice could be connected to a 6th sense, that produced psychic abilities, but he didn't believe that he himself had any.

<Don't be an ass. We need to find her and give the bloody thing back.>

"We would do just that if you could give me something more than 'She wants it back badly'."

Albert leaned forward and looked at the necklace once more. 'Leverage,' he thought. He could often handle Jax's crass and belittling attitude, but it usually didn't do him any good and most times, he felt more like Jax was the person and he was the voice inside Jax's head.

He was starting to feel like, with this necklace, he might have a little.

Jax sucked in a breath and cringed. Albert felt it. It was a very strange sensation. He had never in all his years dealing with Jax, "felt" him do anything.

This unnerved Albert and he made a personal note to check with his doctor about a dosage increase or something.

<I don't know.> Jax spit the words at Albert. <Just please don't touch that thing again. Let's just go find her.>

Albert cocked an eyebrow. Jax had never made a more solemn and pathetic request in their entire time together. This necklace changed Jax somehow and while the calm was beautiful, something about the way Jax pleaded was less than desirable.

He felt a little guilty about toying with the necklace a few more times than was necessary.

"Can you at least give me a direction?"

<I don't know...East!> Jack fired back. The grumble in his voice sounding like an animal.

Albert picked up the necklace by the chain and shook off the loose sand and slid it into his pocket, careful not to touch the charm directly.

He had discovered that skin to gem contact was the ticket. He stood up, stretched and looked around the empty beach one more time. He turned toward the parking lot and saw his truck sitting right where he had left it.

He trudged through the sand toward his small white pickup. He noted how strange it was being up this early in the morning, but it was sort of a nice change of pace. Something about being poked with a stick by other people's children was not how he relished waking up in the mornings. Walking away from the peacefulness is always bittersweet.

CHAPTER 2

Jax was mumbling under his breath. It seemed he was either still suffering the effects from the necklace or he was just really pissed off.

The pain he suffered whenever Albert touched that thing set his brain on fire. He recognized the feeling but couldn't for the life of him place it.

He poured through his memories, watching them play like old 8mm movies. Some recent, cases that he and Albert had been on, double speed rewinding through the bad parts. He saw the aftermath of the accident that took Albert's parents lives and left Albert as a young man struggling to figure out what he was supposed to do. He saw how loving and kind they were to Albert, even when they had no idea how to handle his behavior.

Then he saw Sarah and Daphne. The aftermath of the accident that he caused that took Daphne's life, and drove Sarah away from Albert forever. He sighed. His head hung a little lower.

Nothing he was seeing was what he was looking for.

He dug a little deeper. Back to the time that he and

Albert met and became a part of each other. He couldn't find any of it.

He knew it was some time ago, but he couldn't see it. Only blank space and red letters. Blank space for a long time. The next visible memory was Rose. His sweet, lovely Rose.

He grumbled again. He didn't have time to reminisce, even though he could easily stop and remember Rose for hours on end. He needed to back track and figure out where he knew this feeling from.

He knew it was bad, his gut and his head agreed to that. He wanted to keep Albert safe and the only way he could do that was remember why this necklace was so terrible.

He focused harder and ran further and further back in his memory. Then he tried a different approach. He would just have to find "her". The problem was, he couldn't see her either. Not her face, her location, nothing. He wasn't even sure he knew she was a she. The word "SHE" was the only thing that came to mind when he thought about the necklace and who it belonged to.

It was like someone had taken the scenes in the filmstrip of his memory and placed a sheet of white paper that said "She" over certain ones.

He bellowed and shrieked in frustration. The sound reverberated through Albert's head.

Albert nearly wrecked his truck when he heard the sound pierce his ear drums from the inside. He took his hands off the wheel and placed them over his ears. The truck veered toward the curb.

Albert grabbed the wheel and turned it to the left just in time to keep from driving into the light pole.

He steered to the left hard then back to the right slightly less and regained control. He pulled into the next drive way and turned the truck off.

"What the hell Jax! You nearly killed us!!!" Albert yelled. He wiped the sweat from his brow through his hair and back down over his face. He wiped his hand on his pant leg and back over his face again. He sucked in a few breaths and swallowed hard. An attempt to remove his stomach from his throat.

Jax didn't respond.

Albert has a big heart and can forgive a lot. It is probably what led him to starting a finding lost things and private detective business. He was never good at much, but he was better than good at finding and returning lost things. It started out simple enough, but after a while, people started hearing that he had found this thing for so and so and that thing for someone else, and the next thing he knew he was being paid by people to find missing people and stolen goods.

It landed him a lucrative career, but it also landed him in a lot of hot water. When things, like people go missing, it's usually not because they were living a great life or making the best decisions. They were mixed up in some kind of mess that was dangerous and could get them killed. Albert, with Jax's help, could find them, but Albert ended up in a lot of situations that could have resulted in jail time or dead. Jax never cared. Once again, this time it was nearly dead and they hadn't even gotten their first lead yet.

This was too much though. "You don't feel things. You're just a chemical imbalance in my brain. You don't stress or act all weird about stuff, and you never turn down a case. Now you're screaming at the top of his lungs, making noises and speaking in languages I've never even heard before. What the hell Jax!" Albert yelled.

"You gotta give me something more than East, Jax."

There was a long pause before Jax responded. <I don't know anything else. It's all a blank. I don't even know that for sure.>

A mix of confusion and frustration saturated his voice.

Albert reached into his pocket carefully. He thought maybe the necklace was still causing Jax some issues. He was going to pull it out and hang it on the rearview mirror when his finger grazed the gem for a split second.

Jax let out a yowl. <Stop doing that!!!>

"Stop doing what? I have to get it out of my pocket. Maybe that will help. Besides, it's jabbing me in the thigh.

He pulled it all the way out and hung it over the mirror. "What is your problem?"

<Just stop touching it. It bloody stings!>

"Stings? Like how do you mean? I don't feel anything but a buzzing in my head, and silence for a change. Oh wait, I actually can imagine how you being quiet might hurt. You haven't done it in 30 years." Albert laughed out loud at his attempt at a joke.

<I don't know how to explain it other than excruciating. What the hell is that thing?>

Albert wouldn't have believed it was possible, but he could hear it in Jax's voice. It was echoed in the wails and screams of the other voices too. His heart filled with guilt and sank.

"It's just a necklace Jax." His voice calm and devoid of humor. "What can you...feel about it other than pain?"

<Nothing, absolutely nothing Al. It's terrifying.>

Albert thought for a moment. This was his chance to take the lead. If Jax really didn't know anything about it, he would have to find out some other way. He thought for a long time.

"It's pretty ugly."

<Yeah.>

"And old looking. Like it was beat out with a hammer and a pick."

<Sure.>

"The gem is pretty. I've never seen anything that dark of a green before. Have you?"

<Not that I can recall.>

Jax was still reeling through his memories. He knew he had seen it before but couldn't see it now.

He wanted to know what was happening, but it gave him a really bad feeling.

"Maybe we should take it to a jeweler or something and see if they can point us in the direction of who it might belong to."

<Yeah, sure. Let's do that. The sooner we are rid of it the better.>

These words had a little more spring in them.

It was clear to Albert that he would have to do all he could to get to the bottom of this. Jax either couldn't or wouldn't help this time. He would figure it out and get his imaginary friend back to normal. "Let's go to the house and clean up. It's a few hours still before any place will be open."

<Ok.>

The ride to the house was quiet except for the sobs and sniffles that came from the other voices.

Jax was unusually silent. Albert, not being accustomed to the quiet, turned on the radio. The song that was playing was unfamiliar to him, so he flipped through the channels. He had not listened to the radio in so long, he didn't know if he would recognize anything anymore.

Finally, he came across a song that he recognized. He hummed along. "Hmmm hmm come back water...hmmm..." He was nodding his head in step with the old tune as he turned into the driveway.

He carefully pulled the necklace from the mirror and made sure to not touch the charm. He looked like he was carrying a bag full of dirty diapers as he turned the key in the lock and opened the front door to his house.

Once inside, he turned on the light, kicked off his shoes.

His mother was meticulous about dusting when she was alive. She would be ashamed of him for not keeping up and taking better care of the family home.

He blew against the top of the table and brushed what didn't flutter up into the air in a cloud off on to the floor and set his keys down. He kicked the small pile of dust that landed on the floor under the table with his socked toe and shrugged.

He walked over to his father's old recliner and sat down. He laid the necklace on the table beside him. He leaned back and rubbed his thumb and finger on either side of the bridge of his nose and let out a large, noisy yawn.

"I guess the nap on the beach was not enough. I'll think about where we should start when I wake up. You talk quietly amongst yourselves and see what you can come up with. We will talk again when my eyes open."

He waited for a moment to see if Jax would respond. He didn't. He was still mumbling and ignored Alberts statement.

Albert closed his eyes. A moment later, his head tilted to the side, his mouth hung open, and quiet snores drifted out of him.

Jax mumbled and cursed and agonized over his missing memories until the sun came up.

<AHHHHHEEEEEEEE!!!>

The sound of Jax's screech echoed through Albert's head and he sat upright, grabbing the arms of the chair to steady himself. He patted himself down to find the necklace and get it off his skin.

It was still lying on the table next to his chair.

"What the fuck Jax!!! You could have given me a heart attack. What's wrong!!!"

Wails and cries poured through Albert's skull but Jax didn't respond. Albert huffed and yelled again.

"Jax, what is wrong with you?" The anger in his voice was overwhelming and the cries dissolved into whispers.

When Jax still didn't respond, Albert sucked in a long breath and held it while he counted to ten.

"Jax, answer me or I will pick up that damn necklace again!" The words barely made it out of his mouth when Jax yowled

<NO! PLEASE DON'T. THE MEMORIES. THE MEMORIES, THEY'RE GONE!>

Surprised it had worked, Albert sat back, a little relieved. He exhaled slowly and calmed himself before speaking again.

"Ok, hold on. What memories and what do you mean gone?"

Whining, Jax answered, <Of the necklace. I should know. I should see, but they are gone!> Another yowl was followed by sobs.

Albert had never heard anything so sorrowful and broken. He had no idea what to do. He sat back in his chair and ran his hand through his hair. He blew out hard and spoke again.

"Ok, Jax. Let's take it a step at a time. If they are gone, how do you know they were there?"

Jax settled and tried to calm himself. He had never been so emotional and at a loss. He was terrified. He didn't know how to survive without his memories. <The pain. I know it. I recognize it, but I can't find where I know it from. The memories, the movies that would tell me, are blank. They just say She.>

"Ok, so we figure it out. We are detectives of a sort. This is what we do. We will figure this out. Relax."

<Relax. RELAX!!! MY MEMORIES ARE MISSING AND YOU WANT ME TO RELAX! I CAN'T RELAX, I HAVE TO FIND THEM. I HAVE TO REMEMBER THEM!>

"And you will. We will get this sorted. What do you remember?"

<I remember Rose. My dear sweet Rose. I remember running, and I remember you. WHY CAN'T I REMEMBER THE REST?>

"I don't know why. Maybe if we find this, She, we will get answers. Let me think a minute."

Albert put his head in his hands and started piecing what he knew together.

This was the part he was good at. Figuring out the puzzles

that Jax through at him. "We found the necklace on the beach. It's ugly and bulky, and kind of...relic-y?"

He sat upright. "Relic-y. That's it. The gallery downtown. It has a bunch of stuff like this in the window all the time! We can go there and see if they can point us in the right direction.

<Whatever, let's just go!>

CHAPTER 3

Albert parked on the east side of the capitol building and walked the half block to the gallery.

He stepped out of the truck and turned to lock the door but saw the necklace still hanging from the rearview mirror.

He opened the door and reached back inside. His large frame prevented him from leaning in and simply grabbing the chain, so he had to slide back into the seat.

"I'm going to try to do this without touching it Jax, but I can't make any guarantees. I'm not going to carry it through downtown like it has the plague, so I'm going to slip it into my pocket. Are you ready?"

<Put it in a fucking box or something!> Anger filled his words this time. <For that matter, toss it out in the street and let the trolleys have their way with it.>

Albert was confused. "What about the She that wants it back?"

<She can go out in the street and pick up the pieces if she wants it.>

"What about h...What the hell is wrong with you Jax? When we left, you wanted to get your memories back. Now you want to toss our only lead into the street and let cars run it over?"

<I don't know. I don't like the feelings I'm having right now. Returning it might not be the right thing to do.>

"Returning it is what we do Jax. It is what pays the bills, puts food in my belly, and gas in our ride. Why would we not return it?"

<Just shut up and put it in your pocket. I don't want to watch this anyway.>

"Watch what?"

<I don't fucking know. I can't see it. I can feel it, but I can't see it. Just...lets go already.>

Albert stood up and held up the necklace to look at it one more time before he slipped it into his pocket. The reflection of the sun off the hood of his truck shone just right into the emerald and blinded Albert.

He covered his eyes with his arm. Surprised by how bright the silver-green beam of light was. The thought crossed his mind that when he could see again, he would be in strange place surrounded by aliens. He chuckled at the thought.

He grasped and pulled the outer edge of his jeans pocket open. He maneuvered the chain so that the gem dangled just above the opening and slid it down into his pocket. He shook his leg gently, forcing the gem deeper into his pocket to make room for the bulky chain. The stone pressed against his outer thigh through the thin fabric of his pocket.

Albert noticed an ever so slight buzzing in the back of his head and the voices were subdued, but not completely gone, as before. Albert turned away from the truck and headed toward the gallery.

When he arrived, the door was open, so he stepped inside. Something deep within him made him cover his pocket with his hand. He rubbed the gem gently against his leg as he stepped toward the glass counter in the corner.

The buzzing in his head picked up slightly and the voices in his head stopped completely. He looked around but found no one in visual range. He looked over the glass counter for a bell to ring. There wasn't one.

He decided to browse around. It looked like a standard art gallery, except all the pieces were old, worn, and what he still thought of as relic-y.

There were paintings and sculptures all around him. There wasn't a symmetrical placement of anything.

Columns jutted up out of the middle of the floor, blocking what would be the natural flow of the room. Strategically, it made sense, he thought. A person walking through would have to step around the column and could get a better view of the sculpture on top of it.

He didn't know why someone would want to get a better view though. It looked like was covered in strands of twisted burlap. It had a musky odor to it as well. He turned his nose up and moved toward a piece in the opposite corner of the room.

He couldn't shake the feeling that he was being watched. Every which way he turned, it felt like multiple sets of eyes were focused on him.

Albert spun around and scanned his surroundings. There were video cameras in every corner, pointed at different areas of the room. There was no one else present by him, so he shrugged the feeling off.

He turned to head back to the glass counter, but as he took his third step, he heard a thud behind him.

His gut and his fists clenched as he spun around, expecting to see someone standing there, ready to fight. Instead, he spotted a blue door. It stood out against the bright white walls of the gallery like a sore thumb, but he hadn't noticed it before. It was barely open a crack.

He stood absolutely still and tilted his head toward the door, listening.

Suddenly, there was a loud crash on the other side of the door.

Thinking someone might have fallen, he darted to the door and swung it open. The room was dark as pitch. He plunged his hand deep into his pants pocket and pulled out what he considered the best multipurpose tool, a zippo lighter. He spun the wheel of the lighter just as he stepped through the door.

He shoved the flame into the dark room.

He didn't see anyone. He waved the lighter around the room, watching and listening.

At the back of the room, he saw a flash and then a shadow move against the back wall. He inched his way in that direction.

His skin tingled and it made his stomach flop.

He moved slowly to the back wall and the spot where he saw the flash.

There was no one there. A strange thing happened, though. A scene flashed right before his eyes.

He watched with wide eyes as an arm came from behind him wielding a long, straight object at him.

He dodged it and spun around with his elbow out. He countered the attack and shoved the person to his left. He immediately straightened his arm and caught the offender with a punch in the face. They flew backward into a shelf then dropped to the ground.

Just as Albert was noticing that there was no sound of heavy objects crashing to the ground where the shadow had hit the shelf and knocked several things to the floor, another arm swung at him from the opposite direction. He ducked, and the punch missed him. He stretched out his leg and landed a powerful kick to the second shadow's midsection. The shadow ninja landed hard on the floor, but again, no sound.

A foot flew at his head. He caught it mid-air with both hands and twisted his body. A third shadow figure spun in the air and landed flat on his front, like a belly flop. Still there was no sound. Albert sucked in a quick breath and the room flashed.

He shook his head and looked around, confused. There was no one else there. "That was interesting." He looked around again for anyone but saw no one.

"Jax. You did you see that?" There was silence.

Albert shrugged. As he turned to go back toward the door, he came face to face with a hooded individual with a large metal statue in his hand. The shadow monk swung the statue at Albert's head. Not quite like he had just seen but very similar.

Albert ducked and came up with an elbow to the guys face. He heard a swishing sound behind him and turned to find another hooded individual throwing a punch at him. He dodged and brought his leg up, catching them in the gut.

The third hooded individual came flying at him feet first. Albert grabbed one foot and twisted, like he had seen in the vision. The force he came at him with snapped Albert's arm backwards causing him to wince. Albert raised his arm and slammed it down into the middle of the guy.

He didn't wait to see if there were any others. He dove toward the sliver of light coming from the gallery. He rolled to his feet and bolted out the door. If he'd learned anything from being in the wrong place at the wrong time throughout the years, when you have an opportunity to get out, you get out.

When he reached the brightness of the gallery, he paused for a moment to catch his breath. He thought he was free. He was wrong.

A man in a uniform grabbed Albert and slammed against the wall. He slapped a pair of handcuffs on Albert's wrists.

"Caught ya!" A dickish chuckle followed the words. Long hands attached to lanky arms grabbed Albert and shoved him face first against the wall.

CHAPTER 4

"What? No! They are in there!" Albert turned so that his stretched-out fingers could point toward the door he had just come through.

"Shit! Kovach nodded to a second officer "Hold him." Then he headed into the dark room, gun drawn.

Albert stood there, arms secured tight behind his back. He was proud of himself for stopping whatever had been going on in there. They would be arrested, and he would be free to go.

He was still reeling from the fight he had just escaped from when the officer, Eric Kovach, came back through the door, holstering his gun.

"Alright, turn around." He grabbed Albert harder than he had to and shoved him against the wall. He frisked him. When he found the strange shape in his pocket, he patted it. "Get me a bag." The short round officer that had been holding him darted out front door of the gallery.

"I can explain that." Albert proclaimed as Kovach's gloved hand reached in and pulled the necklace out of Albert's pocket.

As soon as the necklace left Albert's possession, Jax

shrieked. The sound echoed painfully through Albert's head. He tried to bring his hands up to cup them over his ears. His sudden movement startled the officers and earned him an elbow in the ribs. Albert winced.

Helpless to cover his ears, the searing pain of Jax's screams raged on. Albert's ears began to ring. The officer spun him around to face him.

"Start explaining."

Albert couldn't hear the officer over Jax's screams. He hung his head, trying to hide the tears in his eyes.

Kovach, accepting his slouch as guilt, turned him toward the door. The short, round officer came in waving an evidence bag. He handed it over. "Put him in the car. I'll bag this and be right there. I doubt we are going to get anything out of him here."

The second officer nodded and led Albert to his car. He was gentler than Kovach was. Albert was grateful for that.

As the officer placed his hand on top of Albert's head to ease him into the back seat, he noted Albert appeared to be in pain.

"Are you alright?" the officer asked.

Albert only heard the last word. The screaming subsided and Jax voice bellowed with cursing and questions.

<About god damned time Al! What the fuck took so long?>

"Yeah I'm fine. Am I under arrest?" Albert asked the officer.

"Oh, yeah, I need to read you your rights. You have the right to remain silent, anything you say..."

The officer's voice trailed off as panic started to flow through Albert's veins like tiny shards of glass.

"What about the other guys?" Albert interrupted.

"What other guys? Detective Kovach didn't find any other guys. So, sit back and relax. You can tell the whole story downtown. Do you understand your rights as I have explained them to you?"

<Hold it! Arrest? Other guys? What the hell happened Albert!>

"Yes sir." Albert waved his hand. "I choose to remain silent."

He and the officer rode in silence all the way to the station. Jax was blundering through a plethora of questions that he would just have to wait to get an answer to.

Albert quickly thought through everything that happened. They weren't going to believe him. Especially not after finding the necklace in his pocket. He didn't know if belonged to the gallery or not, but it didn't matter. He was caught coming out the back room, in a gallery that had, from the sound of it, been robbed before. He was toast.

CHAPTER 5

Albert sits in the interrogation room. The stale air dries his throat. The cold metal of the table and chair cut through his clothing and send a chill down his spine. He stares at the double-sided mirror across from him mulling over his predicament and playing scenarios of how this could go on repeat in his mind.

Jax is asking questions, making declarations, and cursing at top speed. Albert ignores him as best he can. Only pinching his nose between his finger and thumb when the chaos reaches a fever pitch.

There was a knock on the door and the room fell silent. A familiar face came in, carrying a file folder as thick as Albert's arm. Albert crossed his arms, inhaled deeply, shook his head and exhaled slowly. Jax went back to screaming. Demanding to know what was going on. Albert has learned over the years to ignore him when he's being questioned by Kovach. He doesn't need to appear crazy on top of guilty.

"So, you know what I have here then?" asked the detective as he slams the file down on the table.

"Are we really going to do this again Kovach? Even with all of that, you've got nothing."

"We are going to do this every time until you stop ending up here in my interrogation room. I've not been able to nail you in the past. I have you dead to rights this time though. Don't I?"

"No, you don't. I mean, I know what it looks like, but it's not what you think it is." Albert was almost ashamed of his use of the cliché, but whatever worked. He had no idea how he was going to get out of it this time. They had him dead to rights from their perspective. He felt completely hosed.

Kovach wanted to play the game of cop winning the day. Albert didn't have time or the patience for it. He piped up. "Look, it's like this. I found that necklace on the beach, where I slept last night. I went to the gallery to see if they would know who it belonged to..."

"Let me stop you right there. You slept on the beach again? We have talke..."

Albert interrupted, "St. George Island. Not your beach so move on."

"I see. I assume someone saw you there?"

"The hotel security guard that I talked to...and unless someone has been murdered, it's irrelevant. Let's move on."

Kovach nodded defeat for the moment.

"Anyway, I found the necklace because I was sleeping on it. I took it home until I could figure out how to find its owner. Have you seen the necklace? It's huge and ugly but looks like something a rich nobleman would wear. I gave some thought to what place would have stuff like that. The gallery came to mind. "

"How did you know about the gallery?"

"Are you serious? It's on the strip, downtown. Who doesn't know about it?"

"Had you ever been there before?"

"I pass by it on my way to lunch a few days a week. What the hell kind of questioning is this?"

"Inside, had you ever been inside it before today?"

"No, why would I? I'm not exactly an art connoisseur."

"Ok, so why were you inside today?"

Albert sucked in a long deep breath. "When I got there, the door was open, so I went in. I didn't see anyone, so I browsed around for a minute, thinking they might be in the back or something."

"Did anyone come out? How did you end up in the back room?"

Albert exhaled. "I heard a thud."

"You heard a thud?"

"Yep, then a crash."

Kovach wiped his hand down his face. You heard a thud, then a crash. In the back room?"

"Yeah. On the other side of the door."

"So, you?"

"I ran in there. I pictured this little old man trying to take something down from a shelf that was bigger than he was, and it fell on him. So, I ran in there."

Kovach nodded. "Okay. What did you see?"

"Nothing."

"Nothing?"

"Yeah, nothing. It was dark."

Kovach pulls an evidence bag out of the file and shoves it at Albert. His zippo lighter is in it.

"Then explain this?" Kovach asks as he tosses the bagged lighter on the metal table. It lands with a loud clang.

Albert explains. "It was dark, and I didn't know where a light switch was. I used my zippo to look around, make sure no one was hurt, then find the light switch." He blew out a long breath. "I never go into a dark place totally blind."

"Go on."

"I pulled my zippo out and lit it. I pushed it ahead of me further into the room so I could see."

"What did you see?"

"A flash of light and then a shadow moved against the back wall. I went to it, but there was nothing and no one there."

"So, you left and that's when we caught you?"

"No, that's when I saw the vision."

"Here we go. You saw a vision? When did you eat the mushrooms?"

"Now you are just being a dick. You know I'm clean." Albert pointed at the file on the table.

"I saw the fight, before it happened."

"Fight. What fight. You never said anything about a fight."

" I never said anything. I came through the door to get away from them and you guys grabbed me and threw me in handcuffs."

"Who were 'they'?"

"I don't know who they were. It was dark."

"So, you have no idea who they were or what they were doing there?"

Albert jumps to his feet. His chair slams against the wall behind him. "No Kovach, I don't know who they were. That is your job. I don't have time for this. I'm not going to sit here and do your job for you. Let me know when you find out."

Kovach jumps to his feet and grabs Albert by his shirt. "You just need to confess, and we can be done with this. We caught you in the gallery, with the necklace. and no one else was there."

"Then lock me up if you have everything you need to put me away. You don't. You need a confession, and you aren't going to get one from me. I don't know who they were. Now let me go."

Kovach curled his fists in Albert's shirt and started shaking him.

There is a knock on the door and a leggy woman with cropped red, curly hair stomped into the room. "Let him go Kovach. He's telling the truth."

Albert and Kovach both stare at the woman with their jaws on the floor. She is an older woman, but her classy look; green slacks, a black sleeveless turtleneck sweater and heals that would make a window washer afraid of heights, commands their attention.

Kovach growls. "How the hell do you know?"

She gives Kovach a do you really want to question me look. "Let go." She growls back.

Kovach lets go of Albert with another growl. He turns to leave but the woman glares at him and nods her head at Albert. "Fix his shirt and apologize."

Kovach glares right back at her but turns and pats Albert's bunched up shirt smooth, and picks up the file he brought in. "I apologize. You got lucky. Again." He stomps out of the room.

Albert just stands there, dumbfounded and staring at the woman. "Where have you been for my last twelve run-ins with him?" He asks sarcastically.

"If that was a where have you been all my life line, it was weak." The woman chuckles as walks over to where Kovach was standing and extends her hand to Albert. "I'm Beverly Shaw, the owner of the gallery. First, I want to thank you for disrupting whatever was going on at the gallery. Thank you."

Albert nodded his head. "I'm just glad it wasn't a little old man in the back room hurt."

"Well, the video cameras corroborated your story. I would have been here sooner, but I had to check them first. Where did you find the necklace you were telling Kovach about? You said St. Augustine?"

"Yes ma'am. I was sleeping on it."

"What made you think to bring it to the gallery?"

Albert was embarrassed to answer her question when he thought about his first assessment of the necklace. He hesitated but didn't know what else to say. "It kinda matched the things in the gallery. I thought if it didn't belong there someone there might have an idea of who it did belong to."

"I see. Well, thanks for finding it. It does belong to the gallery. The video shows that you aren't responsible for either robbery, so you are free to go."

Jax starts going crazy inside Albert's head. <Who are you talking to Al? Don't tell me this mess has you really talking to yourself. Tell me what is going on!>

Albert puts his hands up over his ears when Jax lets out a screech. <Her! She! My memories!> Jax wails.

CHAPTER 6

Beverly yells. "Shut up Jaxolox!"

There is a loud crack in the air and Albert stiffens. Jax and the other voices in his head stop talking immediately.

"You can hear him?" Albert asks.

<She can hear me?> Jax repeats the question.

"Yes. I can hear him. Annoying as ever." Beverly answers.

Questions start to pour out of Albert like a waterfall.

No one else had ever acknowledged Jax before. The called Albert crazy, told him he was hearing things, and was medicated. He wanted to know how she did it. He was confused, but more in awe.

Beverly stops Albert's verbal dribble with a wave of her hand.

"That's not important right now. I need to get you out of here and I need you to come and show me what you saw in the gallery. Let's go." She stands up straight, walks through the doorway, and waits for Albert to follow.

Albert stands there, staring out the door after her, not realizing she expects him to follow her. No interrogation ever has gone like this one had. He had no idea what to do.

Beverly steps back into the room and asks "Unless of

course you want to stay here. Shall I send Kovach back in?" Albert snaps out of his stupor and bolts to the door and follows her out.

"You're that detective guy that finds the lost things, right?"

"Ummm, yeah. That's me. You lost something?"

"Yeah, the necklace for starters. I don't know what else yet. That's why I need you to come with me back to the gallery."

They stop at the evidence counter and collect Albert's belongings. There is a hold up because Kovach has not returned with the evidence bags yet. The girl behind the counter tells Albert to take a seat. She'll call him when she has his belongings.

Beverly shakes her head and huffs. "Just stay right here."

Albert looks at the girl at the counter and back to Beverly and shrugs. He swings his arms and starts whistling quietly. Jax is going nuts inside his head. He ignores him.

Beverly pulls out her phone, presses a button, and puts the phone to her ear. "So, we are in the habit of detaining non-criminals around here by not bringing their belongings back to evidence?" She nods her head while a tiny inaudible voice comes through the speaker. "I see. I also don't care. Tell him to get it back here now. The longer I wait around and see the shape this place is in the more I start to regret my investment." She hits a button the phone and drops it into her pocket.

She winks and smiles at Albert. "We will be done here momentarily." She walked over to the missing people board and started making a note of who some of the new ones were and what probably happened to them.

Albert was stunned. He stood there beside the evidence window and just stared at Beverly. Jax took the opportunity to chime in with his thoughts on Kovach and Beverly. Cursing abounded and it was all Albert could do to tune him out.

After a few minutes, the woman behind the window returned with a large yellow envelope. She slid a clipboard under the glass and told Albert to sign it.

Albert looked at Beverly. His gut told him not to sign anything until he had ALL his things back. He now knew who it belonged to and he wanted to be the one to return it to her. He got paid better that way. He sent a questioning look in Beverly's direction.

Beverly returned an understanding nod and then looked at the girl and Kovach. "The procedure is to make someone sign that they received their belongings before actually receiving them, then?"

Kovach sucked in an angry breath. "Not to the best of my knowledge." He nodded at the young woman behind the window. "One sec." Kovach reached into his pocket and pulled out Albert's zippo lighter still in the evidence bag and slid it into the envelope.

Albert was given the envelope. His anxiety hit its peak until he looked in the envelope. He gave it a slight bounce and shifted the ziploc bag containing the zippo. Beneath it was the necklace. A smile spread across his face.

Jax screamed. The sudden sound made Albert's head throb. He shook his head and brought one hand up to his ear. He poked his finger in his ear as the sound continued. He looked up and noticed everyone staring at him. He took his finger out of his ear and shrugged. "Tinnitus. It hits me out of the blue sometimes."

He happily signed the form. "Can't say I'm sad to be leaving. Can we get out of here now?"

Beverly nodded and waved her hand, gesturing for Albert to lead the way. She nodded at the detective as she passed by him. Her nose slightly pointing skyward. "Good day Kovach."

Kovach took a step backward and gestured her toward the exit. There was a buzzing sound and a click as the metal gate shook and shifted on its hinges and swung open. Albert took a few steps and stopped.

"Where's my truck?" Albert asked.

It should still be where you left it should it not?"

"It should be, but they like to make life difficult around here." Albert and Beverly both turned and looked at Kovach for an answer.

Kovach nodded. "It is right where you left it."

Albert and Beverly nodded and made their way outside.

When they got outside the precinct Albert apologized for being adamant about making sure he had everything. "Kovach and I go way back, and I slip through his fingers every time. Getting away from him again will just drill the thorn in his side that much deeper."

"I can see that. Have you had many run ins with him before?"

"A few. I'm a private investigator. I'm in a lot of places at the wrong time, and he is the lead detective. I end up being a suspect at first, a lot. It doesn't help that I've solved a lot of his cases for him. It makes him bitter."

"I see. What kinds of things do you investigate?"

"I find lost things and return them. Kinda like this." Albert starts to pull the necklace out of the envelope. His finger grazes the emerald. Jax bellows, curses and then grumbles "bitch" under his breath. Albert drops the necklace and pulls his hand out of the envelope.

Beverly arches an eyebrow. "What's wrong with Jax?"

"I don't even know. He's goes crazy screaming and screeching every time I touch the necklace. Can you pull it out of the envelope? He's really giving me a headache."

Beverly reaches in and pulls the necklace out without saying a word. Jax falls silent. She pulls the necklace out of the evidence bag and holds it up in front of her. "Oh yes. I remember this old thing." She lets out a sinister laugh.

"So, you can hear the voice in my head. How?"

"Yes. I hear him. He's annoying as hell. I don't know how you've stood to live with him all this time. I'm so sorry." She looked away and scanned the parking lot for her car.

"Why did he shut up when you told him to?"

"There is power in a name, I know his, and he has to do what I tell him to."

"What? You...KNOW a voice in my head?"

"We go way back. He's not just a voice in your head Albert. You know that."

"I know no such thing. He's a voice I've been hearing since I was six. I'm on medication for it and everything."

"And that's made the voice go away?"

"Well no. It helps with anxiety, but they haven't been able to find a drug that makes the voice go away."

"They never will." Beverly's head snaps sideways and she looks directly at Albert with a strange gaze. "You never told him Jax?"

Jax remained silent.

"You asshole. You let this poor human believe he was crazy his entire life! I've got your number Jax." She yelled at Albert.

Albert brought his hands up to defend himself against this old woman that looked as though she could stab him in the forehead with her stiletto before he even knew what happened. "What are you talking about?"

"It's not important right now. We need to get back to the gallery. You find lost things and I have a job for you if you want it."

"I'd take it, sure, but I don't know how helpful I'll be right now. Jax is my search engine and he's on the fritz right now."

"That explains a lot."

"What do you mean by that?"

"It makes sense. Jax is the god of lost things. Or one of them, at least."

Albert laughs out loud as Beverly walks toward her car. Albert stops laughing when she shoots a serious glance over her shoulder at him. She hands the necklace back to him. "Come on. We have work to do." He trots to catch up with her.

When they reach her car, he goes to the passenger side and reaches for the door as it pops open. He nods and slides into the seat. He holds the necklace up. "I found it on the beach. Is it yours?"

"Yeah. It's mine."

"Holy hell. He found you and he wasn't even trying. So, why does he go crazy when I touch the necklace and why couldn't he tell me anything about you?"

Beverly sighs. "I don't have time to explain it all right now. Let's just say, he was forbidden to so much as speak my name or have anything to do with anything to do with me. He probably gets zapped anytime he tries." Another sinister laugh escapes her.

Albert was confused again. She made no gesture to reach for the necklace and instead, put the car in reverse and peeled out of the parking lot.

Albert harumphed. "So, wait. I don't understand. He is forbidden? You realize you are talking about a figment of my imagination not being allowed to do something, right?"

She laughed. "Oh Albert. Has he really not ever told you anything?"

"Anything about what?

Beverly patted his hand that was still holding up the necklace. "Hold on to it. It's safe with you." She wiggles her fingers and it and whispers something under her breath. "It will help keep you safe now."

Jax shrieked. <Take it back you foul witch!> Jax's voice boomed through Albert's head like a drum.

Albert scolded him. "Be polite. You are talking about a lady. The one that saved my carcass this time, no thanks to you."

Jax harumped. <She's no lady Al.>

"Just shut up! What do you mean by protect me? Do you mean like it showing me the vision in the gallery?"

"What vision?"

"The one that I had about the fight with the shadow monk ninja guys right before they attacked me for real?"

"You knew about that too?"

"About what?"

"The necklace protecting me."

He expected her to chuckle like Kovach had when he described his attackers. Instead, she said "Oh... NO!" She pressed the pedal to the floor.

CHAPTER 7

Beverly pulled up in front of the gallery, threw the car in park and jumped out before Albert realized they had even stopped. She rushed to the gallery door and slid the key into the lock. "Come on! We don't have much time!"

Albert maneuvered his large frame out of the front seat and sauntered to the door.

"We need to figure out what was taken now!" The urgency in Beverly's voice made Albert feel a little uneasy. He followed her inside anyway.

She led him straight to the door of the back room. When they got there, he stepped in front of her. "I'll go first. Just tell me where the light switch is?"

She reached around the corner beside him and flipped a switch and the room flooded with light. After a moment of blindness, his eyes adjusted, and he could see into the room in all its cluttered glory.

There were rows of tall metal racks along one wall that filled most of the room. A row of folding tables along the other. He took a few steps into the room, searching for a door out in the back somewhere.

"What are you looking for?"

"A door. When Kovach came in, he said there was no one here. If no one came out before me, and there was no one in here after I left, there has to be a door."

"There's no door."

"There's no door? Then how did they get out?"

"Teleportation spell." Beverly said.

Albert wasn't amused. The look on Beverly's face was all serious. "As a heart attack."

"You can't be serious. A spell? Do you really expect me to believe that?"

"I don't know what I expect you to believe, but I believe it. There was no other way for them to get in here. Even then, with the wards I have on this place, I don't know how they got in at all. I need to figure out who they were and what they took."

Albert's blood boiled. "I don't think this is funny at all. You ask me for my help, bring me back here, and then tell me the bad guys got in and out using a spell. I thought I was the crazy one." His anger reached a fever pitch. "I'm out of here." Albert turned and headed out of the room.

"Wait. Then how do you explain the shadow ninja monks?"

Jax laughed out loud. Hearing the words shadow ninja monks roll out of her mouth was hilarious. The boisterous sound rumbled around in Albert's head.

"What? What did I say?"

Albert was too angry to laugh. He growled instead and kept walking toward the gallery. "So, I imagine things sometimes." He grumbled under his breath.

"Like the one you call Jax, hmm?"

Albert shot her a glance. His response was cold and

clinical. "Jax, is the result of a chemical imbalance in my brain. The shadow ninja monks must have been also. I don't have any other explanation for it. You said you needed my help. Instead you just want to be an asshole and make fun of me."

Beverly couldn't help laughing out loud. She stopped suddenly when she noticed the look on Albert's face. It was sad and down trodden. "You're serious? You really believe that Jax is a chemical imbalance?"

"What else would he be?"

"A demon."

Albert stormed out of the room and into the gallery toward the front door without another word. Beverly ran out after him. "Albert wait!"

Albert kept going. "Wait for what? For you to laugh at me again? No thanks."

"Albert. Stop. I really need your help. I'm having trouble wrapping my head around the fact that you don't know what Jax really is. I'm not making fun of you."

Albert stopped cold. "What Jax really is? You are going to try to convince me that he's a scary monster from the depths of hell that eats children and rapes women in their sleep, and he's in my head? You aren't making a very good case for me to stand here and listen."

Beverly stopped. She looked at him pleadingly. "I...I'm sorry. I don't have time to explain it all right now. I didn't realize that you weren't aware or how strongly you believe that he's a... disease. I really do need your help, right now. I can explain it more later, just, right now there are much more pressing matters."

"More pressing matters? Like what?"

"Like, the end of the world."

It was Albert's turn to laugh out loud. "The end of the world? Look lady. The things you have in here are ugly and probably worth a fortune, but I highly doubt any one of them, or all of them for that matter are going to start World War three."

"I'm not talking about a war Albert. I'm talking about things you can't even imagine being unleashed on the world. Otherworldly things."

"Bullshit. There are no such thing as otherworldly things."

<That isn't exactly true Al.>

"Shut up Jax! I can't even deal with you on top of this craziness right now."

"Albert. Otherworldly stuff does exist. This gallery is full of it. You don't have to believe that if you don't want to, but I need you to believe the possibility does exist just long enough to help me figure out what was taken. After that, whatever you want to go on believing is totally up to you. Just, please, help me figure out what is missing?"

Beverly's pleading wasn't working.

<Al. She's right, and she does need our help.> Jax pleaded too.

"Are you for real Jax? First you tell me we can't trust her, we need to stay as far away as possible. Now, you are trying to convince me to stay and help her. What are you trying to pull here Beverly?"

"Jax. You are going to have to prove it to him."

"Prove it to me? What can he possibly do to prove to me that he's not a figment of my imagination?"

Jax audibly sucked in a breath. Albert felt it. The room

around Albert and Beverly started to shake. Albert felt a strange vibration stir in the center of himself. It grew stronger and faster as it radiated out. Albert's mouth opened and a loud and unfamiliar voice bellowed out. "There are things beyond your current comprehension Al. I've been wrong to keep them from you. Help Beverly and we will explain it all later."

Albert dropped to his knees. The sensation overwhelmed him. He could feel Jax inside him suddenly. Like he was in a pitch-black room where he couldn't see anything, but there was a presence there. He could feel it clearly enough to see it.

A fearsome and ugly creature looking at him from the inside out. Horns spilled from the top of its head. Red gleamed from its eyes and spilled down its face like streams down a steep mountain. Its skin was scaly and wreaked of burnt flesh. It reached for Albert as it spoke. "Tell her what you remember."

"Stop!!!" Albert yelled. This was way too farfetched for this strange woman to pull off just to get him to help her. "What kind of magic is this?"

"That isn't magic. That's Jaxolox. The god of lost things. A demon. This is magic." Beverly twirls her hands around themselves and chants something. A strange ball of light forms and shines out brightly between her fingers. She shoves her hands at Albert and the ball of light flies toward him.

He tries to duck away but the light hits him. He slinks away, expecting to be burnt or disintegrated into nothingness. Instead, he's filled with comfort. A warm softness he can't explain forms around him, and he feels safe and relaxed.

"Whoa." Albert sits there for a moment reveling in the intense feeling.

"Now, would you please follow me back in here and tell me about the monks?"

Albert nodded his head and stood up. The whole place looked different but the same. The pieces on exhibit were alive. Things were moving in them, but Albert wasn't afraid. He followed Beverly through the blue door.

"What do you see now?" Beverly asked him.

The room looked drastically different. All the items in it were the same, but now there was color. "Strips of color."

"Color? Ok, what colors?"

"Overall, blue. There is a stripe of green that seems to be attached to every relic in here, like a chain."

"Ok. Good. Anything else?"

"Yeah. There's red. Weird, zig-zagging lines of red everywhere."

"Ok. Where does the red come from and where does it go?"

Beverly watches Albert attentively as he walks to the wall at the back of the room. He presses his back to it for a moment and then steps forward, very methodically.

"They came in right here and went this way. The searched through these boxes right here. Then these one's over here. They froze right here, then they were all over the place." Albert moved through the red lines all around the center of the room. Albert stopped and his eyes met Beverly's. "This is where we fought. I can see the lines of the fight. Whoa."

"Good. Keep going. Can you see anything else?" Beverly coaxed.

Albert looked around the room. He took three large steps toward the door to the gallery. "They started to go this way, but then turned." He turned toward the back wall and ran to it. "They ran back through the wall right here. Whoa."

"Okay. Good. We know how they came in and how they left. We also know that they fought with you. Close your eyes. I want you to tell me what they looked like."

"Shadow monks that moved like ninjas."

"Specifics Albert. I need details. What were they wearing? What did their faces look like?"

"I don't know. They were probably figments of my imagination. In the vision, they just looked like wispy smoke shadows."

"If they were figments of your imagination, you would be able to tell me everything about them. They were real Albert. Focus. What did they look like? I need to know what they looked like and what they got away with."

"Can you not just check your inventory?"

"That would take months. There are a lot of demons trapped here, and in 3 other warehouses around town. It will take forever to go through each one and track down a single item."

"Are you sure they only took one?"

"Oh Shit!" Beverly screeched. "I really need to know what they looked like Albert. Concentrate. What were they wearing? Could you see even a glimpse of their face? What did you smell?"

Albert closed his eyes. He inhaled deeply. Pulling the scene up again in his mind. He saw the darkness and let it seep over him. He thought about the feelings he was experiencing, pulled the sights, smells, and sounds around him. He recalled a rustling sound, the smell of dust and moisture, and dirt. He didn't think that information mattered, until Beverly asked him what he smelled.

Suddenly he saw it. The statue coming at him. He concentrated and focused on the item coming at him in his mind. He paused the scene and examined the statue. He described it. "They tried to hit me with a trophy. Or it looks like a trophy. Hang on. An Oscar? It was bronze and long and thin. He swung it like a bat."

"An Oscar? Like the movie award trophy?" She walked over to the row of shelves to Albert's right. She lifted the lids on a few totes and shifted some paintings around before finding what she was looking for.

"Yeah, like that, but not an Oscar."

She held up a long and slender statue. It was a sleek black cat shaped piece with gold paint that defined the cat features. Expensive looking bright green gems were centered in gold circles for eyes, a small yellow circle stone was affixed to its forehead and a blue diamond shaped stone stuck out of the middle of its neck. She asked if it was something like this.

"A cat." Albert turned his head toward her and opened his eyes. A surprised expression moved over his face. "How did you know?"

"Witches intuition".

That was the last straw for Albert. His brow furrowed and his glare threw ice daggers at her. She shrugged off his icy stare. He didn't have to believe that she was a witch. Right now, they needed to concentrate on figuring out what had been taken. "Concentrate!" She yelled at him.

Albert huffed. He closed his eyes and moved through the rest of the encounter. He mumbled and she searched through the shelves until she heard him say something that made her stomach sink.

Albert was recalling his fight with the second shadow ninja monk. "The second monk. He had a red spot in the very center of his hood. It was a long black hood. It pulled tight at the shoulder. Holy shit! They had faces!"

Beverly chortled. "What does that mean?"

"I thought they were just shadows. That was all I saw in the vision. Wispy, smoke like shadows. after the vision, in the real fight, they had faces. The one I kicked in the gut actually had facial features. A chin and a nose were all he saw, but they were there. They were solid."

"Solid, like stone?"

Albert chuckled this time. "No, they were squishy, muscular but squishy. What kind of monk would be made of stone?"

"There is a faction of monks in the Himalayas that can merge with stone. They can move into and through stone. That could be how they were able to be here when you were in here but weren't when Kovach came in."

"Or, Kovach was in on it. He said he didn't see them, when he actually did. "He told them to lay low and he would come to let them out later." That, to Albert was a much more plausible explanation.

Beverly rolled her eyes at him. "Then where are they now? We just left Kovach at the station. He didn't look like he was in any kind of hurry to get back here and let anyone out."

Albert wanted to disagree. He really couldn't wrap his

head around any of this. He had to keep going though. He never quit a job. He wasn't about to start now. "Let me see."

He got quiet again and mumbled to himself as he twisted and turned through the motions of the fight. His moves were less than graceful. His shoes slid and scuffed on the slick, painted concrete floor. He tilted and wavered on one foot, almost falling over as he kicked one leg up into the air. He righted himself quickly by flailing his arms to and fro to regain his balance.

Beverly tried to contain her laugh but was unsuccessful. The vastness of the room quickly filled with her loud guffaw.

Albert stopped suddenly and turned to her with a scowl. "I'm no kung Fu master. I'm trying though. Do you want to know more or not?"

She laughed for a moment longer, allowing herself to enjoy the entertainment and not feel guilty. She apologized when his icy glare hit her again. She took a deep breath to regain her composure and motioned for him to continue. She snorted and cackled once more and then quickly put her hand over her mouth. She apologized again. She kept her hand over her mouth and stared down at the floor. She waved her hand in a circle. "Go on."

Albert centered his mind again by taking a few cleansing breaths. He closed his eyes and continued his dance with the shadows. Beverly choked and coughed behind him trying to hide her laughter. Albert ignored her and continued. He stopped suddenly. "They work slick bottomed shoes! No treads!"

"How in the hell is that helpful?"

"How many monks do you know that wear shoes at all?"

"Several." Beverly shrugged. "Is there anything else?"

"They were black."

"The monks?"

Albert rolled his eyes. "No! The shoes."

"Their shoes aren't helpful Albert. Look at something else."

"What do you mean the shoes aren't helpful. How many people do you know that would want to break into your gallery wearing hoods and black, slick bottomed shoes? It's not your normal robbery attire. The hoods are on long, black, almost shiny robes, with red dots on them? Surely, there can't be many."

"You'd be surprised. What can you tell me about the red spot? Was it a symbol or just a red spot?

"It was a symbol. I don't know how to describe it though. Round, wavy lines and straight lines."

"Could you draw it?"

Albert chuckled again. "It will be rough, but I can try?" He looked around the room. "Shall I use a chisel and a block of stone, or do you actually have paper and a pen in this relic dump?

Beverly wasn't amused. She punched him in the arm gently as she walked past him. "Follow me." They walk to the glass desk in the gallery. She pulled a pen and paper from a shelf below it and handed them to Albert. He started to draw.

As Beverly watched him draw her eyes grew wide and panic spread through her. "Are you absolutely certain that was the symbol?"

"It's not a work of art worthy of your gallery here, but it's a good start.

"Holy mother of Jesus and Batman! Shit!" Beverly cursed out loud and ran back to the storage room. By the time Albert caught up with her, she was on a ladder twenty feet in the air above him, frantically digging through a crate. She continued to chant "Shit shit shit". Her voice echoed through the room.

"Shit what? Beverly? What's wrong?"

She prayed and then cursed again "Oh God. Shit shit shit. It isn't here. We must get it back now! She jumped out from the ladder and seemed to float rather than fall, at a great speed.

Her heels clacked on the floor in front of Albert. She marched up into his face and began to yell. "Jaxolox! Where is the statue of Dongorul?"

CHAPTER 8

Albert stepped backward and brought his hands up to defend himself. "Whoa! What the hell are you talking about?"

<She's talking to me Al. Directly to me. Brace yourself. I'll handle it.>

"Jaxalox! Where is Dongorul? I command you to answer me.!"

<I will you crazy bitch. Stop scaring the guy. Jesus!>

Albert chuckled. For a moment he forgot that she could do that. It was funny to him. Funnier still that Jax would curse using Jesus. "Yeah. Okay."

<Back the fuck up lady. You are making an awful lot of demands with no answers of your own.>

"I know your name. I've used it. Now do as I command!"

<I don't know where Dongorul is. Haven't seen him in at least a hundred years. Nasty that one. Why would I want to know where he is?>

"Don't play games with me demon. I need to know where he's been taken before they free him."

<Ooohhh. That does sound like a problem. I don't know where he is though.>

"He's missing. You must know where he is. Now tell me or I'll permanently bind you to that necklace!"

Albert stood there, eyes wide and mouth gaping. Speechless. His brain toiled with what was happening. He questioned, did she just call him demon. Is Jax a...demon? No, he argued with himself. He is the result of a chemical imbalance inside my brain. Why would she call him something else, though? Why would he respond? What the hell? These were questions that plagued him.

Albert's legs began to shake and grow weak. He dropped to his knees. He stared up at Beverly. Albert tried to speak. His mouth formed words, but his own voice does not follow them. The demon was taking over.

Jax's voice morphed and boomed from Albert's lips. <I shall not.> He hissed at her. <I am the God Jaxolox, the finder of lost things, and the commander of legions. I do not answer to the whims and fancies of beasts with breasts. It is I who should command you.> The words thundered through Albert's head. Echoed by a choir of high pitched and scratchy voices. The words trumpeted out of Albert's mouth and resounded throughout the room around him.

"Calm yourself demon. We are in trouble here. I mean no harm, only to stop whatever is going to happen with Dongorul. It was I who called you forth and I who released you from your prison. It is I that will put you back if you don't cooperate." Beverly's voice was full and commanding. Attempting to use the power of his name to regain control.

<It is you, demon hunter, who tricked me and trapped me in the body of a small child. Why should I cooperate with you?>

<If he was missing, I would know it. He's not. Go ahead and bind me to the necklace, if that is what you want. I won't be able to help you convince Al here to help you if you do.>

Beverly, assuming that she had the demon's attention and willingness to cooperate, relaxed slightly. She sucked in a deep breath before answering. "Because the apocalypse is upon us. The statue that is the prison of Dongorul has been stolen. I need your help to find it, determine their plans for it, and to stop them."

Albert jumped to his feet. "Okay. Stop this! Apocalypse, Dongorul, Demons? This has gone far enough. Why are you treating my disability like a joke? I'm appalled that someone of your caliber and upbringing would be so callous and ridiculous."

Before Beverly could respond, Albert stomped over to the shelf where he set the large yellow envelope. He pulled out the evidence back containing the necklace and tossed it in the air toward Beverly. I've returned your necklace. Thank you for choosing Suadade Agency. Please consider using our service again should you lose anything else. Have a nice day." He tucked the envelope under his arm and stormed out.

Beverly lunged forward and caught the necklace just before it smashed into the floor. Although it looked strong and well made. It was far from indestructible and the power it contained was not to be handled lightly.

She landed flat on her belly with a smack. Her arms stretched out in front of her, barely keeping her chin from bouncing off the floor. She opened her eyes and her hands as she sat up. The necklace was safe. She exhaled a sigh of relief and despair as she watched Albert storm out of the room.

The demon had clearly not told him his story. 'What a horrible thing to do to a man.' She stopped and imagined for a moment how she might have handled learning these things the way that he is. She has taken her knowledge of other-worldly things as a given. She mentally chastises herself. She has always known of them. Coming from a family of witches and learning the ins and outs of demon hunting before she could walk.

She felt bad that she assumed that he was taught, as she was, about these kinds of things. She didn't have time to explain things to him, though. She needed his help and he was going to have to deal with the newness of it, or they would all die. She rushed out after him.

She called out to him before he reached the exit of the gallery. He stopped but didn't turn around. He was already having a hard time fighting the anger at her treatment of him. He couldn't bear to have her do it again. "Fool me once," he told himself.

Beverly spoke gingerly. Apologizing for her behavior before. She was not aware that he was ill-advised by the voice in his head all these years. She understood it, now, and would be happy to explain it. Time was running out though and she desperately needs his help.

Albert accepted her apology but turned and walked out of the gallery anyway.

CHAPTER 9

Albert walked the few short blocks to his truck. Trying to ignore the chorus of panicked voices in his head. Jax had remained silent while the others mumbled and whined about exorcisms and agonizing bindings. Albert couldn't shut them out. As he continued to hear words like Master, apocalypse, and Dongorul, his anger grew to boiling.

He shoved the key into the lock of Ol' Blue and slid into his seat. He leaned his head back against the headrest and rubbed the bridge of his nose between his fingers. "Shut up!" He yelled at the voices with every bit of anger and sincerity he could muster.

Jax finally spoke. <I didn't have a choice Al, she summoned me, I had to.

Albert shushed him too. He didn't want to spend another moment thinking about it. He was done with this particular case and would hear no more about it. Albert ran his hand through his hair and down the back of his neck before slipping the key into the ignition.

Jax, in true fashion, refused to let things go. He had allowed Albert to believe that he was just a figment of his imagination for all these years. A blink of an eye to Jax, but a lifetime for Albert. Jax had enjoyed the time with Al and was starting to see the damage he had actually caused him. They were all in trouble now, and he needed Al to believe and help him stop the devouring one.

He started to explain things to Albert. <So, when you were young, I was already over a thousand years old. I don't know what happened, but suddenly, I was inside you. You were so young, and I had no idea how I had gotten there, but I felt safe. The last thing I wanted was to be exorcised, so I hid. I pretended to be an imaginary friend to avoid detection. I'm not a bad guy Al.>

Albert slammed his hands against the steering wheel. "I said I didn't want to hear any more about it. I have a mental disorder. It causes me to hear voices. I take medication for it, and apparently, I need to go see my doc and get something changed. I will go ask him to give me the heavy stuff. You will go away, and I can live some kind of normal life...as a medicated zombie.

<I am not a hallucination. I am a demon!> Jax's voice boomed through the truck, rattling the windows. Medication has never worked Al. No amount of it will. You were a small child when I was forced into you. I had no desire to harm you, so I convinced you that I was just an imaginary friend. Everyone had one. I let you believe that I was nothing more than a voice. The time has come for you to hear and understand.>

Albert didn't want to hear anymore. "I've really heard enough of this bullshit for today Jax. Give it a rest. Albert put the truck into drive and rolled toward home.

Jax was far from finished. He asked Albert, <What makes it bullshit Al? It's not like medication has ever worked. You

can't shut me up, and you have trusted me for 30 years now. A mental disorder is treatable. I am not.>

Albert stopped listening. He shoved his hand in his pocket. He was going to squeeze that stupid necklace as hard as he could. He was tired of hearing about this. He didn't want to talk or think about it anymore. The world as he knew it, his world, was supposed to be in danger. He wanted answers, but not the one's he was getting. Right now, he just wanted silence and a chance to think.

The necklace was gone though. He was back to being stuck with Jax's meanderings and moans. He regretted giving it back. It was the only thing that in 32 years that had ever silenced the voices. He desperately wanted it back right now.

He yelled at Jax. Just shut the hell up already!" Albert pounded the steering wheel. I don't care what you are. I just wish you were gone!"

<Whoa, why don't you tell me how you really feel. Why would you say something like that? I've been so good to you Al. Why would you want that?>

Albert balls up his fist and punches the steering wheel. His anger was getting the better of him, but he couldn't keep quiet any longer. "Good to me? You have been good to me? How can you even say that Jax? Being in constant trouble with the law, Daphne and Seralie, my parents, that's been good to me? That was good to me Jax? I'd hate to see what you would do if you were bad to me."

<You don't mean that! You wouldn't dare!>None of that matters now. You don't know what's at stake right now. None of it is going to matter if Don...>

Steam physically boiled inside Albert's brain. He sucked

in a breath and sucked in another one. His nostrils flared and his face turned a deep shade of red. Albert interrupted him. "Don't even say it Jax. What part of I don't give a fuck if the world ends tomorrow are you not understanding. I don't care if it comes in the form of all the volcanoes in the world going off at the same time or Cthulhu wakes up and devours us all. I'm done!"

<You don't mean that. Beverly asked for our help. We can't just abandon her in this.>

"Why can't we? We found the necklace and returned it to her. In return, she insults me and makes fun of my...condition. Why would I ever want to help someone like that? She can afford to find someone else. Or you can go. You are the one who always figures these things out anyway."

<Who else was there? Who else saw them? Twice? I've never known you to be the type to just walk away when someone needs help Al. It's been the key to our success.>

"What more help does she need? I helped her figure out who was behind the robbery, and she paid me with insults."

Jax sucked in a breath and thought quietly for a while. When he finally spoke up, his voice was soft and solemn. <She wasn't trying to insult you. She was assuming that you knew more about the situation than you actually do.>

"What is that supposed to mean?"

<That means that she has been dealing with this kind of stuff for ages, probably centuries at least. She assumed that, since I am a part of you and I have dealt with it, that you have been too. It shocked her. It doesn't matter though. What she is facing affects all of us. Human and demon alike. If we don't help her Al, we are all going to die.>

Albert sat quietly for a long moment. He had helped her figure out who took the necklace. What more help could he be? He didn't believe in witchcraft and wizardry. Even less so in demons. He believed in angels, but only because he had to believe that was what had become of his mother and Seralie. Demons and the apocalypse, though? That was going too far.

"We did help her."

Jax could tell that this was not the way he was going to get through to Albert the seriousness of their situation, or, after they saved the world, destroy the bitch that did this to Albert. He changed his tune.

<Don't you want to know how she knows my name? How she was able to hear and address me? You are not the least bit curious?>

"I don't care how. She will keep trying to convince me that demons and all that nonsense exist, and I don't believe any of it. It would be pointless."

<But we do exist.> Jax was becoming angry. Albert could claim ignorance all he wanted, but the words were powerful. It wasn't that Albert's words could cause him, and others like him, to no longer be in existence, but they could do damage all the same. <What about all the movies?>

Albert froze. Then he laughed hysterically. "Movies? Really? We want to challenge my beliefs and use movies, figments of someone's imagination made into a reality of sorts by using props and visual effects, to make your point?" He laughed again. "That is the most absurd persuasion I've ever heard you use. I'm not possessed Jax. I have never crawled backward up a wall or across the ceiling. I don't vomit pea soup, and I don't care what you say. You are not a demon."

Jax chuckled. <Do you need to crawl across the ceiling to be convinced? You aren't possessed. Only bound. It's different. >

Albert's heart sank. After his experience with Beverly and Jax earlier, the thought occurred to him that maybe that was possible. That was the last thing he wanted. His stomach started to turn. "No. And I don't want to vomit pea soup either."

Jax bellowed with laughter. The noise filled Albert's head and echoed like it was a large, empty cavern. He sat there. A disgusted look spread over his face as the understanding of Jax's statement sank in. "So, how much of what I see in movies is actually true?"

<Well, honestly, it's probably a fifty-fifty split. This isn't like that though. Those are over takings, possessions, if you will. The people in the movies portray events that happen when a demon takes over the body it inhabits. This isn't like that. We share this space, but I have no control over it.>

"So...wait...what? How is that possible?"

Jax let out an almost agonizing whine. <This is going to be harder than it looks. I don't have time to start at the beginning Al. Just know this. I am a demon. There are many like me. We exist. Beverly is a Phareli She's an old demon huntress from a long line of demon hunters. She's not a demon, but not a human either. We (demons) exist to make life miserable for you humans, the Phareli keep us in check, otherwise, we would easily destroy the world. Making sense so far?>

"Yeah, I get that."

<Ok, good. Here is the hard part. It gets all confusing and

I don't even know how it works. There is power, and there is magic. Two different things. Right?>

"Ok?" Albert agreed but didn't understand.

Jax exhaled and thought for a moment. <Ok. A guy pulls a rabbit out of a hat. What is that?>

"Illusion."

<Alright, maybe this will be a little easier for you to understand than I thought. Most people would call that magic. It's not.>

"Well, I understand that some things like that, Magic Tricks, of that sort are illusions. I've seen a lot of shows about that too."

<OK, so then there is power. It's an ability to manipulate energy and make things that wouldn't ordinarily happen, happen. That is power. That is what I have. Power. I can make things that wouldn't normally happen, happen. Do you follow me?>

"I think so. What is your power?"

<Think of it as a...spidey sense about things that are lost.>

"Oh, right, ok. I follow you now. Your super power is being able to detect lost things. That is how we are able to never lose a case. It's a superpower. You're a...superhero?"

<Hell no! I wouldn't be a super hero if you paid me.>

"You're a super villain, like Magneto then?"

<By the gods you watch too much telly. No. I'm not like a supervil...ok, hold on. Maybe this is helpful. I'm more like the incredible hulk. Do you know that guy?>

Albert burst out laughing. "You are big, green, and like to destroy things? That's fantastic!"

<What? No! I'm harmless. Misunderstood, but harmless, unless provoked.>

"Then you turn green and start breaking stuff?" Albert laughed at his own joke.

<Ha ha. No. I mean I suppose I could. Never tried it. No. I'm like him in the sense that I'm pretty lax and laid back until necessary. Then, when something is lost or missing, I change.>

"You kick into hyper mode and can't stop until it's found?"

<Exactly. It's more than hyper mode though. It's chaotic and dangerous. I'm not always a good guy Al. I've been pretty good to you, because I've had to be. In reality, I'm a terrible friend.>

"What does that mean?"

<We can discuss that later. Right now, we need to focus on helping Beverly.>

"Please stop saying her name. I'm done with that. I've helped her all I'm going to and that is the last I want to hear about it. I'm driving this boat and this boat is going home. Got it!" Rage was building up in Albert again.

<Ok. You've been through a lot. Let's go home and get some rest. I need to think in peace.>

Albert growled. "You...you need to think in... Jesus fucking Christ! I'm done." They rode the rest of the way home in silence.

CHAPTER 10

The drive the rest of the way home was quiet. When Albert got there, he sank into his recliner, feeling lost and alone. He forces himself to think about other things, pleasant things, like puppies and cotton candy. He closes his eyes and fades into a pleasant dream.

He shoots up out of his chair like a rocket when the sound of glass shatters behind him. It wakes him from a deep sleep. He spins around and sees a shadow move across the kitchen.

He hunkers down in front of the recliner and grabs the bat that lays beside it as home defense. He gently brushes the dust from it and holds it tightly. He slowly looks sup over the top of the chair and peers into the darkness.

The shadow moves slowly toward him. Albert watches. It is a body, of that much he is certain. He ducks back down in front of the chair and plots his next move. His heartbeat thrums in his head, drowning out any other sounds. He inhales deeply in an attempt to calm himself. He turns his head and listens for the footsteps approaching him. "Now is not the time to panic". He whispers to himself.

He turns toward the front door and attempts to judge the distance in the dark. It's too far for him to make it there before the shadow would be on him. He looks the other direction toward the fireplace. In the corner, between the hearth and the corner is the darkest spot in the room. He creeps toward it and crouches as low as he can.

He lingers there, watching and waiting for the shadow creature to show itself. <What the hell is going on?> Jax yelled.

Albert nearly jumps out of his skin. He falls sideways and drops the bat. He knocked a tall metal vase over. It lands on its side with a loud clang, revealing his location to the intruder.

Albert picks the bat up as he jumps to his feet. He swings it and connects with the intruder's head with a solid "thwack". As the intruder flies backward and lands on the floor, Albert watches and confirms it is another shadow ninja monk. A thought occurs to him. "These guys aren't very good ninjas."

Jax laughed out loud. Albert is certain that the neighbors probably heard him. Albert watches for the hooded man to move. When he doesn't, Albert strides to the lamp on the end table and turns it on and returns to stand over the hooded man.

<Hit him again.> Jax demanded.

Albert didn't hesitate. He swings the bat down on the cloaked head and waits for him to move. When he doesn't, Albert bends down and feels around on the man's neck for a pulse. It didn't take long for him to find a strong one.

Albert wipes the sweat from his brow and acts quickly. He grabs the man up and hoists him into the recliner. He turns the light on in the kitchen and rummages through a couple of drawers. He hurries back to the recliner with a roll of duct tape and 20 feet of rope. He quickly binds the breaker inner in the recliner.

When Albert is satisfied that the intruder is secure, he steps back and looks him over. He slips the hood off his head. "He doesn't look much like a ninja."

Jax laughed out loud again. <What should a ninja look like?>

"I don't know. Asian?" Albert laughed out loud this time. He turns his attention inside his head again. "Don't ever yell at me like that again Jax. You scared the shit out of me, and he could have killed me because I was more focused on you."

<How was I supposed to know we were under attack?>

"I don't know. It was dark and I was crouched in a corner with a bat in my hand, maybe?"

Jax ignored his question. <Well now what do you plan to do? You have him subdued, right?>

"Yeah, I think he is out cold, but alive."

<Slap him!>

"What?"

<Slap him. We need answers. Slap him. Wake him up and get them.>

"Jax. I've already pinged him with a bat. I'm looking at assault. Do we really want to slap him to wake him up?"

<Ugh! You dolt. The end of the world is nigh, and you are concerned with criminal convictions. He broke into your home and attacked you. Get the bloody answers. We will worry about the rest later. Slap him!>

Albert examines the man tied to his recliner. He isn't dead. He lets Jax's statement sink in for a moment. 'This guy did break in, and I highly doubt it was to invite me to a tea party.

Jax is right. We need answers.' He leans over the man and pats the him on the cheek. He spoke in a quiet voice.

Jax bellowed. <What are you doing? Slap the ever-loving shit out of him. We don't have time for coddling!>

The booming voice startled Albert. He pulls his open hand backward and let it fly. The back of his hand connects solidly with the man's cheek. A stinging buzz radiates up Albert's arm. He grabs and rubs it with his other hand as he watches the stranger come to.

There is a stirring, then stiffness, and then a shaking of his head before he opens his eyes. 'This is no ninja.' Albert thought to himself. His confidence in his having the upper hand here grew.

The man shakes and hops around in the recliner trying to free himself. His eyes dart around the room until they land on Albert standing solidly before him.

Albert ran his hand through his hair. Twice already today he had been assaulted. This guy was here to do it again, and here he was trying to be nice. Albert shook his head in disgust with himself.

<Question him!> Jax shouted.

Albert nods and turns to his left. He paces back and forth in front of the recliner, recalling the several times he's been interrogated by Kovach. He sucks in a breath and then speaks boldly. "Let's start off easy. Who are you and what are you doing here?

The man looks around the room again. His eyes searching for something. When his eyes land on Albert this time, they scrunch up in the corners. His brow narrows, his lips sneer and a guttural sound escapes them. He continues to struggle under the ropes as he inhales and exhales deeply.

He pressed with all his might against his bindings. The rope stretched and creaked, but the duct tape held firmly.

"Hmmm. Doesn't look like that's going to work. Duct tape is an amazing invention, don't you think? You aren't going anywhere, so you might as well answer my questions."

<That's it Al. You are in control. Get what you want from him.>

The man looks around once more and then lets his shoulders slouch and relax back into the recliner. He growls again but this time is was less guttural. "The holy one will get you for this. He will swallow your soul." He spit at Albert.

Jax laughed out loud and the sound echoed through Albert's head. Albert brought a hand up to his ear to stop the echo. <Who is the holy one?>

"Who is this holy one?" Albert asks in a demanding tone.

The man's face twists into an evil grin and a loud obnoxious roar of laughter spills out of him. His bald head presses back into the soft fabric of the recliner. He stops laughing and silence fills the room. His head snaps forward and his gaze meets with Albert's. He opens his mouth and the words flow from him like a lion's roar.

"The devourer of souls. He will come for yours."

Jax pftted. <There are thousands of them who claim to be soul eaters. Which particular one is he speaking of? Go on Al, ask him which one.>

Albert mirrored Jax's expression of pfttt. "There are many who claim to devour souls. Can you be more specific?"

The almighty Dongorul. The ruler of them all."

The mention of the name shook Jax to Albert's core. <SHIT!!! WE NEED TO CALL BEVERLY. NOW!!!>

"What? Why her?" Albert asked Jax.

The man closes his mouth and looks at Albert with a questioning gaze. "Dongorul is no female. He is the 7th Horseman of Hell. You know nothing and you will die an ignorant fool."

"I thought there were 4 horsemen."

Jax laughed out loud again. <There are hundreds of horsemen. The one that he speaks of is the 7th in the order of horrible things they can do. Call Beverly now!>

It was Albert's turn to have a go at the confused look. Jax's response didn't settle him any. He asks. "Why?" with his back turned, he spoke in a whisper. A habit he picked up over the years to avoid looking like he was talking to himself.

<She will know how to deal with him and his holy one.? Jax had no rhyme or reason to whisper, but he did.

"How bad is this guy?"

Jax chuckled. <Oh, now you want to know. I thought you didn't believe in this kind of stuff.>

"I'm fighting shadow ninja monks in my own house so I'm giving it some more thought. How bad?"

<Well, he is known as the devourer of souls. He and I hold the same rank, in the scheme of things, only I'm a good guy and he's...well...not so much.>

"You're a good guy?" Albert laughed out loud.

<Well, considering, yeah. When was the last time I demanded that you sacrifice a puppy?>

Albert cringed at that. "He does that? Alright, so what should we do?"

<We take him to Beverly.>

"Seriously? What good will that do?"

<She will know more about his followers, where we can find them, and maybe, if the fates are kind, tell us how to stop them.>

Albert starts to sweat. He couldn't tell if it was the thought that he was going to have to accept this demon nonsense or that Jax was scared and he could feel it, but he didn't like it.

"So, how am I supposed to get him back to the gallery?"

<I don't know. Knock him out again and throw him in the trolley? You are the one with the physical form. You figure it out.>

"Can't you, like, take over him and make him walk, or something?"

<You really have watched too many movies Al. Do it!>

Albert sighed. "Alright, we can do this one of two ways." He turns back toward the man in the chair. "I can carry you awake or unconscious. Which is it gonna..."

<HIT HIM!!!He will fight you if he is awake.>

Albert swings the bat without hesitation. It connects with the side of the man's head with a loud crack. "He is going to have matching lumps on both sides of his head when he comes to again."

<Probably a concussion too. He'll be alright, and if he's not. Well, he shoulda thought twice before breaking in here.> Jax replied.

"True. I'll consider it paying the cost of the window he broke to get in here. Remind me to get that fixed later?" Albert still felt a little guilty. He made sure the man was out cold and leaned in to hoist him up over his shoulder.

<I'm not your secretary Al. Take off one of his shoes and leave it here.> Jax ordered.

"What? Why?" He didn't hesitate to talk to himself now.

<So, he doesn't try to run.>

"How long has it been since you had a physical form Jax? You can still run without shoes."

<Yeah, but it's an awkward run, until you get rid of the other shoe. That gives you an...just fucking do it!>

Albert drops the man back into the chair and starts to untie his right shoe. "This is ridiculous." He drops the shoe on the floor next to the chair and lifts the body up again. The man is light for his size, Albert thought. He hefts and bounces him on his shoulder and walks toward the door.

He stops and steps back to the table next to his recliner and picks up his phone. He slipped and slid his finger over the screen several times but doesn't find what he's looking for. "Shit. I don't have her number."

CHAPTER 11

Albert sped quickly through town. Making the easily thirty-five-minute drive in just under fifteen. He pulled into a parking spot directly in front of the gallery and spied Beverly standing at the glass desk with a customer.

He went inside and stood patiently for a moment, waiting for Beverly to acknowledge his presence and hurry this other guy along. When she didn't, he cleared his throat. The sound echoed through the gallery. It was an obnoxious sound when it reached his own ears the third time.

Beverly looked over the man's shoulder and shot Albert an angry glare. He knew right then that talking to her was going to be as much fun as taking a long leisurely stroll on shards of glass. He then thought maybe taking that stroll might be more pleasant.

When she still did not acknowledge him, he started waving his arms and gesturing to get her attention so he could mouth to her why he was there.

She looked up at him and stifled a chuckle. His movements, as graceful as they were, were clumsy and when she finally did see him, he was trying to keep a sculpture and a bust with a necklace on it from toppling over. She laughed out loud.

When he heard her laugh, he turned his attention back to her. He started gesturing that he had a guy tied up in the truck and needed to talk to her. Now!

When he noticed the customer was also looking at him, he froze. He had gotten as far as gesturing that there was a man by holding his hand was near his crotch like he was holding his penis in his hand to specify male. His other hand was pointing to his truck.

Beverly cracked up. Albert slowly dropped his arms to his sides and shoved his hands in his pockets. His face turned a deep shade of red as Beverly leaned back against the wall and cackled.

The customer shook his head and turned back toward Beverly. She tried to get a hold of herself. She apologized to the man standing in front of her. He leaned in and whispered something to her. She lost it again.

She cackled and howled as she nodded in agreement to whatever it was that the man had said. The man turned toward the door, nodded at Albert and then shook his head has he pushed through the glass door and out of sight to the right.

Albert stomped over to the glass desk and waited for Beverly to pull herself together. When her laughter did not stop right away. He cleared his throat again and then spoke. "So, I have one of them in the back of the truck. What do we do with him?"

Beverly's eyes went wide as she started to choke. She pounded on her chest with a last laugh. "You what?" She stood there staring at him, waiting to hear the rest of the story.

"He broke into my house just a little bit ago and attacked me. So, I clubbed him with a bat and tied him up. Jax said we should call you. I don't have your number, so I threw him in the back of my truck and came straight here."

Beverly's jaw was on the floor. "Why did you bring him here?"

"Where do you suggest I should have taken him? To Kovach? I was going to, but Jax insisted I bring him here instead. So, what now?"

"Jax? What does he think I'm supposed to do with him?"

"I don't know. Interrogate him, I guess. I tried but wasn't able to get much more than the holy 7th horseman was coming, and he was going to eat my soul."

"The Holy 7th Horseman?" Dongorul is far from holy." She inhaled a deep breath and shrugged then rotated her shoulders. "Let's get him secured in the back room before he wakes up, I guess." She came from behind the desk and beat Albert to the glass door.

Albert threw up the lid of his camper and dropped the tailgate. He grabbed the now struggling man by his ankles and slid him toward him. Not at all cautious of the dirt and debris that was surely cutting and scratching the man in the process. "Am I going to have to hit you again?"

The man stopped struggling and shook his head. Albert grabbed higher on the man's legs and pulled him to a standing position against the tailgate. He bent and placed his head and shoulders into the man's midsection and hoisted him up over his shoulder.

A grunt escaped the man's nose as his weight settled into Albert's shoulder. He carried him inside, through the gallery, and stopped at the door of the storage room.

Beverly locked the glass doors and turned the sign to closed.

She rushed across the gallery and opened the door. The room was dark. She turned on the light and stepped into the room. Albert stepped into the room and they both looked around. When they were certain that the room was empty aside from them, she rushed to the back of the room and grabbed a stool. She carried it over and set it down in front of Albert.

Albert gently lowered the man to his feet and guided him as he sat down on the stool. He held on to him as he adjusted himself and was stably seated. He reached up and pulled the hood down, exposing the bald and now badly disfigured head. The man squinted as the bright lights of the room glared around him.

"You don't get out much do you?" A jab at the pale color of his skin.

The man didn't respond. He sat there, squinting as the bright light of the room bounced off the walls. He looked around the room. Not seeing anything of real use that could get him out of this, he inhaled and exhaled slowly and hung his head.

CHAPTER 12

"So now what?" Albert asked.

"I don't know. Why did you bring him here? What did you think I could do?"

Albert had no idea. The last thing he wanted to do was get into another argument about demons and the like, but Jax said she would know what to do. "I don't know. It was Jax's idea and he doesn't seem to want to talk much when you are around. He insisted that I bring him to you, though."

The man on the stool looked back and forth from Beverly to Albert and then at the floor. He chuckled.

"He can't." Beverly said.

"He can't what?"

"Jax can't speak to me unless I address him. He shouldn't even be able to be in the same room with me. It must be agony for him."

"Agony? Jax doesn't feel...whoa. He felt the necklace. Why?"

"Because I banished him from me, a long time ago."

"Banished him? What does that mean."

Beverly, also wanting to avoid a repeat of earlier, thought for a moment about how she was going to answer his question. She inhaled and slowly exhaled before responding. "Are you sure you want to know about this? It will challenge your beliefs to their core, and we don't have time for you to have a another melt down because you don't want to believe it." Never one to pull punches. She took a step backwards and waited for his answer.

Albert scratched his head. He didn't. He really didn't want to hear any more about demons and witches, but he had been attacked, in his home, by this guy spewing nonsense about the same things. This meant, to him at least, that Beverly wasn't the only crazy one in this case.

"Yeah, I guess I'm as ready as I will ever be. I don't want to believe this shit, but this guy was in my house, dressed just like the guys that attacked me here earlier. Something is going on and I won't be able to do anything else until we get to the bottom of it. So, yeah, what does it mean?"

"It means I cast a spell that made it so that he cannot so much as speak my name without experiencing pain."

Albert took that in, swished it around in his head, and let it steep a moment. "So, that creates so many questions. Where do I start."

"Let me break it down for you. I'm a witch. I am almost 300 years old, and I am a demon hunter. I trained for over a century to be able to smell, hear, and sometimes even taste demons. It is my job to capture and imprison them when they sneak into this realm. I'll let that sink in a moment."

Albert nodded. He took the information and thought about what that meant. He was standing next to and talking with the oldest person he has ever met. She didn't look a day over forty. "So, how is it that I ended up with Jax?" The sarcasm that rolled out with his question was palpable.

"Yeah, that...that was an accident. A mistake I will not make again. I had no idea where he had gone. Had I known, I would have fixed it immediately."

"So, you could fix it?"

"I can."

"So why don't you?"

"More pressing issues at the moment, I suppose. That and the fact that it's not a simple snap the fingers and he is gone process."

The man on the stool sat up and cocked his head to the side. He shot Beverly a questioning look. "Fixed it? He is blessed with the internal presence of a God, and you would fix it?"

Beverly shot a look back at the man. "He isn't a God. He is a demon. He needed to be put away for his crimes, just as your demon is."

Jax interjected. <Well, actually. I am.>

Beverly and Albert both shouted at Jax at the same time. "Shut up Jax!"

"He will not be for much longer." The man rolled his eyes away from Beverly as he spoke and stared off into the darkness at the back of the room.

"What does that mean?" Beverly and Albert asked in unison.

The man looked back and forth between them again. "The holy one will be returning for us soon. We shall revive him from his sleep in that stupid statue and he will reward us."

Jax howled with laughter. <Your reward will be death. He

will eat you because eating you is the only thing that matters to him. Some reward!>

Beverly took 3 long strides and met the eyes of the man on the stool. "Revive him? It took me years to put him there. You will not revive him!" Her nostrils flared.

Albert placed his hand on her shoulder and pulled back gently. "Hold it. You put him in a statue? How the hell does that work?"

Beverly spun on her hills and glared at him. "Are you dense?"

Why do you guys keep asking me that? No. I am highly intelligent. Top of my class in school, lucrative business owner and yada yada yada, but this kind of stuff is new to me. So please, stop asking me that, and humor me with an explanation." Albert's response more demanding than sarcastic.

Beverly checked her anger. She inhaled and exhaled slowly. "Ok. Crash course in demonology. There are demons. They are everywhere. They shouldn't be, but there was a loophole in an ancient plan, and here they are. It is my job, well my other job, to collect them when they get out of hand and imprison them in artifacts. I store the artifacts. That is job two"

Albert followed the course and swished the information around for a moment. When the realization hit him, he shouted. "Wait a minute! This place is full of demon prisons? And you display and sell them? Like art?" Albert glared at her this time. He still wasn't sure about the whole demons and possession thing, but this was almost disgusting to him. "So, so Old Lady Dimock could be waltzing around the next ball with a demon in a glass bubble around her neck? That is kind of awful."

Beverly laughed lightly. "Yes, sort of I suppose. I've never thought of it like that. It is kinda creepy when you put it that way. This stuff is more artsy though. It's extremely old and expensive. It's mostly kept on display under glass cases or hung on a wall in a gallery type stuff. It's kind of like reverse sea monkeys, they are on the inside looking out but can't be seen or heard from the outside. A very specific ritual puts them in and a very specific one will let them out. The stars pretty much have to be completely aligned for the ritual to work."

"Perfectly aligned? You mean like what is supposed to happen Friday night?" Albert's voice squeaked.

"Is there an actual alignment Friday night? Well, that explains the robbery. I'm actually surprised that more items haven't been taken then. Beverly laughed out loud but stopped suddenly when she felt Albert's eyes on her in a hard glare. "Look, I'm a demon hunter. It's what I do and what I have done for a century. They rarely get out after I put them in. It's a gift."

<That's exactly right, Rarely. I've been trapped here for thirty-two years now.> Jax threw in.

"The equivalent of a day in your life span demon. Hush."

<A day in line at the DMV!" Jax squealed. Laughing at his own joke.

Albert shook his head. "Alright, then explain that to me. I'm not art. How did I end up with Jax?"

Beverly took a deep breath, hung her head, and exhaled slowly.

CHAPTER 13

Beverly couldn't hide her bitterness. She refused to. It wasn't often that she had to because most already knew the vile nature of those from the other-world. Jax, at least in her case, was the worst of the worst. He took her Jacob from her. She would never forgive him for that.

"Jaxolox is a demon. A creature with a nature of destruction, hell bent on devastation and vile intentions for humans. Other demons too, if I know him at all. He may have been just a figment of your imagination, but he turned the lives of so many upside down, including mine, before I captured him. "

Albert wanted to roll his eyes at the word demon, again, but as she continued, mentioning destruction and devastation, she had his attention. He put his elbow in his hand and brought his other hand up to his chin. He stroked and rubbed at the stubble. If he was going to help her and stop these guys from attacking him out of nowhere, he needed to know more. "So, how did he end up inside me. Is he bound to me now?"

"The first rule of spell casting is to never do it from an emotional state. The second is use the least amount of energy possible. I went against both. I was angry, the spell was overpowered, and in my haste, I overshot the necklace. As for how he got into you, I'm not certain. Were you anywhere near the apartment over on Moxley and Main about 32 years ago?

"Yeah. My aunt lived there, and she was my sitter until I was twelve. Whoa."

"Really? Which unit?"

"Seventeen, but I played all over the place there. Except for around thirty-two. That area creeped me out after...whoa."

"After you met Jaxolox, I'm going to assume?"

"Yeah. It was weird. This vibration went through me, like I'd stepped on a live wire or something. I never wanted to go near that door again."

"That explains a lot about why I couldn't track him down. I wasn't expecting him to end up inside a person. I'm so sorry. If I had known I would have removed him immediately." Beverly bowed her head. She'd made a lot of mistakes that day and she was finding one more person's life she'd ruined because of it. Determination to stop whatever Dongorul had planned was even more pertinent now.

"So, why did you not look for him after that? Why did you not hunt him down?" Albert asked. Recalling all the havoc that has happened in his life. He wondered if his life would be any different if he had stuck around instead of running home and never going back that day.

"I did. I checked everywhere in the complex that day. And over the next few months, I expanded my search. I watched the mailman and the water delivery guys when they came, just to be sure they had not picked him up and carried him off. I've been searching for him ever since. I didn't know you existed, let alone had been there and ended up with him."

"Would summoning him not work?" I don't know a whole lot about this, but I know that when you summon a demon, they must come. Right?

"Right. Every month on the full moon for the past thirty-two years, I have been. I'd go to the portals and summon him. He wouldn't show. That night on the beach though, I tried something different. Instead of summoning him to me, I summoned him to the necklace.

"Portals? Locations where the magical pull is strongest and the window between here and... wherever, is thinnest?"

"Yes. There is one there on the beach that is thin, and on full moon's, the energy there is intense. I went to that one a lot."

"Whoa. This is blowing my mind. I don't know how to tell you this, because I'm struggling to believe it myself, but we would end up on that beach just about every night after the full moon. Full moons are crazy in my line of work and I would always go to the beach to relax and sleep because it was the only place Jax and the rest of the voices would be quiet. Did you do anything different that night?"

"I didn't think it would matter, but yes. I tried summoning him to the necklace. Nothing else had worked." She went to quietly talking to herself. Drawing lines in the air and making conclusions. "Ha ha, that makes perfect sense."

"You want to share with the rest of the class?" Albert joked.

I didn't undo the protection spell before I cast the summon spell. He couldn't come directly to me because he was forbidden to. All those years ago, I didn't want him sneaking up on my or him knowing I was sneaking up on him, so I cast a spell that would wipe his memory of me, and anything that had to do anything to do with me. He would just feel pain if he tried. He came but had no idea why or to whom. He wasn't allowed to even see me. You found the necklace on the beach because I was there, trying to use the necklace to find and summon him. He didn't appear immediately, so I didn't think it had worked, but here you are."

"I suppose it has. You know where he is now. So why have you not tried to remove him from me and put him in the necklace now?"

"Well, I learned some things."

"Like what?"

"If you recall, you stormed out earlier, taking him with you. He's not been out in the world doing any damage, and you seem to have a decent handle on the thing."

CHAPTER 14

Rage stared to build in Albert. His observed handle on the thing was not a handle on things at all. Little Seralie flashed through his mind. She was on the swing at their favorite park. The summer sun reflecting off her bright blond hair. The sparkling jewels in her bright blue eyes and a giggle that sounded like angels singing rang through his mind. He squeezed his eyes closed tightly, trying to prevent the images that always followed.

Saralie's limp body lying on the bank of the lake in the park. Tears filled his eyes as the sound of Angela's sobs and the image of her holding her daughter's lifeless body in her arms played on loop. The images stirred and heated his emotions to boiling. He wanted them to stop, to go away forever, but they overtook him, and he was powerless to stop them.

Beverly saw what was happening. She backed away from him and spoke to him quietly and calmly. He looked like he was about to have a stroke. The pain in his eyes spoke of a sadness brought on by loos and agony at the hands of the demon. She thought, perhaps, that the demon's crimes were not as minor as she had suspected. She knew that look. She knew it all too well.

She had to press on though. Nothing was going to bring whatever was lost back to him, or her. Even if there was something, it wouldn't matter. They were facing the end of the world now anyway. She needed his help. She needed him to focus.

She needed to intervene before he stormed out again. She placed her hand gently on his forearm and spoke very softly. "I'm so deeply sorry he took something precious from you. I can't change it. I can, offer this though. Having him with you all this time has probably kept a lot of people from getting hurt. I know that doesn't do anything for the pain and loss you have experienced, but if you can imagine the number of people who would have felt what you have and worse had he been free all these years...her voice trailed off. She thought to herself about what little consolation that would have been for her.

It was then that the bald man on the stool slowly stood and rushed passed the two of them. He darted for the door. He had rocked back and forth on the stool until it teetered and tipped over, dumping him to the floor. He got to his feet and ran.

The sound of the stool crashing to the floor pulled Albert from his sorrow filled state. They both jumped out of their skin and turned toward the sound of the crash just as the man was rushing past them. He had managed to loosen the ties enough to run before they even remembered he was there.

"Shit!" Beverly and Albert exclaimed at the same time. They ran into the gallery thinking they had been hot on his heels and catch him before he reached the front door and got it unlocked. He was nowhere to be seen.

They burst through the glass doors of the gallery, Beverly in front. Out on the sidewalk they looked up and down the sidewalk in both directions. Albert went to the left a few paces and Beverly to the right. They saw people walking in both directions but none of them resembled the bald man in a hooded cloak running for their lives.

They met back at the door. "Well, that solves that." Beverly shrugged and turned back toward the gallery.

Albert shot her a questioning glance before following her inside.

Beverly walked back to the back room. She picked the necklace up from the shelf she had set it on earlier. She headed back toward the gallery and collided head on with Albert.

He put his hands on her arms and steadied her as she bounced off his broad chest and stumbled backward. She righted herself and straightened out her hands to indicate when he could let go of her. He loosened his grip. He knew he was a large individual, but he was in good shape for his size, so the collision was anything but soft. He wanted to make certain she was steady before he let go.

"I'm fine. Take this and follow me." She held the necklace up so Albert could slip his head through the chain.

Jax bellowed as Albert's head bowed to allow Beverly to slip the chain over his head. Albert stood upright, placed his hands over his ears and backed away. "I can't take that. It hurts Jax when I touch it for some reason. Although I enjoy the peace and quiet that it brings, now that I know he is an actual soul, I can't cause him pain."

"What do you mean it causes him pain. Can you feel his pain?"

"No, not exactly and yes. I feel a buzzing in the back of my head, but when I stop touching it, he and the other voices scream like they are in agony. It's agonizing inside my head. He says it hurts. I can't..."

"Oh, ok. Hold on." She turned and walked back into the storage room behind her. She headed to a heavy, dark curtain in the far-right corner of the room. She slid the curtain aside and stepped into a dimly lit space. Albert followed closely behind her.

CHAPTER 15

Albert stepped into the dark space and looked around. He watched as Beverly kicked her shoes off on the concrete floor and then stepped onto the rug. A small space sectioned off by black velvet stretched across wooden racked enclosed the space. An altar of some kind had been set up here. A collection of heavy black velvet curtains had been hung high on the walls and bunched up in piles on the floor. Another curtain of the velvet was draped over a table that was nestled in the corner.

Two edges ran along the wall. It appeared to be shaped perfectly to fit against the corner. It sat on top of a deep dark red colored rug with a gold pentagram weaved into the middle of it. On the table, a row of seven candles, flames flickering, lined the two edges against the wall. In the middle was a large, round, stone tablet with a pentagram in the middle of it and random numbers circled the edge of it. Directly to the left of the slab was a dagger. It had an intricately carved wooden handle. The blade was a very smooth and sharp looking two-sided number. A small cauldron sat toward the left at the top near the candles. A tiny burner of some kind kept the liquid in the pot simmering gently.

To the right of the tablet was a long, tapered wand. It was made from two types of branches, painstakingly twisted together with a narrow length of black silk ribbon. It was intertwined and tied off at the wider end. The extra length of the ribbon pooled on the table beside it. Above that as a goblet. The stand of the glass looked like it was made from a red dragon's foot. The claws pointed upward, and the glass sat neatly between the long black talons. The liquid in the glass was clear. There were various types of stones and crystals spread around the table, and two tapered candles stood directly in the middle between the goblet and the cauldron. They were a dark, blood red, almost purple color. The flames on top of them seemed frozen. The dyd not flicker and dance like the candles in the back.

Albert kicked his shoes off and watched as Beverly carefully and graciously approached the table. "Please step inside the circle and be as still and quiet as possible." She whispered to Albert.

He took a large step into the circle and stood there motionless. Questions riddled his brain, but he remained quiet.

Beverly leaned forward and lifted the necklace up over Albert's head. Albert braced for what should have been the worst noise in his head. Instead, it was quiet.

Beverly turned away from Albert and took a deep breath. She set the necklace down on the stone slab and lowered herself to her knees. She gently lifted the curtain that was draped over the front of the altar. She pulled out a large wooden box and set it to her right. She lifted the lid and began stretching and pulling on compartments until the box was stretched to three times its original size.

Albert folded his arms and stood there watching her lean over the box to take something out and sprinkle it over the cauldron. He listened as she chanted words he did not understand. She did this several times. As she did, Albert noticed the necklace started to glow. With each new ingredient, the glow changed color.

Albert felt Jax start to stir inside him. He couldn't have explained it if he wanted to. Jax was normally nothing more than an irritating noise I his head. Now, though, just now, he seemed to have a presence. Like he was sharing the space with him. Albert didn't like it.

"Stop! What are you doing?" Albert exclaimed.

Beverly shot to her feet and spun around to look at Albert. She placed her hands gently on Albert's arms. She rubbed softly. "I'm changing the spells on the necklace so you can use it without causing Jax any pain. Why, what happened?"

"I don't know how to explain it. It's like, I feel like I'm sharing my body with him now. It hasn't felt like that before. What did you do?"

"Hmmm," Beverly stopped and thought for a moment. "Are you sure?"

Albert shifted himself around a little. The feeling had faded. "NO, I don't feel it now."

Beverly turned back toward the alter and continued her spell casting. "Ok, I'm almost finished, and you should be able to wear the necklace without it affecting Jax. It will give you a bit of added protection from demonic things and negative energy as well."

"Will it still let me see things like it did before?"

"I don't know. I don't know why that happened. It wasn't

something I put into the charm and I don't know of a spell that will do that. Magic doesn't work that way. Are you sure it was the necklace that did it?"

"It had to be. It had never happened before I found the necklace."

"That means the necklace was probably amplifying your own ability. That's interesting. You never had that happen before? Even slightly?"

Albert thought for a long moment. Trying to recall any previous instances that he was able to see things before they happened. Not like this. "Not like that. No."

"You had never been attacked like that before either though? It would be a self-preservation thing. So being attacked would not be the only thing to trigger it. Have you ever noticed, or had a sense of seeing things before they actually happened, no matter how briefly?"

He recalled lots of instances where he could look at a situation and see the probable outcome, but he had never thought of that as visions. "I don't have a psychic ability. That's always been Jax."

"What do you mean it's always been Jax. That isn't one of his powers. He has the ability to sense things that are lost and lots of other things, but even he cannot see into the future. Not even a second."

"I can just think ahead. It's not a special power or anything. I don't see the future. I just think about all the possible outcomes in a situation. It's not the same thing."

"And yet, with the necklace, it appears that it is."

"It's not. Jax has the ability. He is the reason for the business. It's not what I've always dreamed of doing, but we find lost things because He can't stand to know that something is lost or missing. He gets quite irate about it actually. He can only find things that are misplaced though. Things that have been stolen or given away, he can't find. It's weird."

"That shouldn't seem strange, if you realize that he is the God of Lost Things."

CHAPTER 16

"What? What do you mean the God of Lost Things?" Albert asked.

"Really want to know?" Beverly replied.

"Bullet point it?"

"Sure. Three demon levels, plain old run of the mill demon, demi-god demon, and god demon. Jax is the latter and his domain, or area of expertise is lost items."

Beverly added a few more ingredients to the cauldron as she spoke. She picked up a dropper that Albert had not noticed before sitting next to the bubbling pot. She squeezed the squishy end of the dropper and dipped the tip into the cauldron. She stood up, chanted more words and then squeezed the dropper gently. A single drop of liquid sparked as it fell into the tapered candle to the left. She spoke the chant again as another spark came from the candle on the right.

She took a small step backward and watched, whispering her chant. The necklace lifted off the table, like an invisible hand had picked it up by the chain. It hung there in the air. The glow around it ebbed and waned, changing colors as it circulated around repeatedly. A current of electricity spread between the two tall candles on stands and then shot to the necklace. The glow settled on a red color that grew brighter and brighter until it was almost blinding. Beverly picked up the pace of her chant but turned her head to look away from the blinding glow.

Albert watched the glow until his eyes could no longer take the burning. He looked away a second, maybe two, too late. When the bright red light filling the small space receded and the necklace dropped back to the stone tablet, he was blind. He rubbed his eyes and started to panic. "I can't see!"

Beverly knelt and proceeded to close the compartments on the wooden box. "It's temporary. You should have closed your eyes. Give it a minute. You will be able to see again. I promise." She lifted the drape at the front of the table and placed the box back from where she had taken it. She stood up and picked up the necklace. When she turned around, she laughed out loud.

Albert was standing there, eyes wide open, feeling the air. His arms were stretched out in front of him as far as he could reach. His hands alternated between stretched out and wiggling to straight up, fingers pointing at the ceiling. He really was blind.

Beverly approached him and grabbed one of his arms and led him back to the bright lights of the storage room. He tiptoed behind her, still feeling for the surroundings blindly. When they reached the openness of the storage room again, she let go of him and went back into the makeshift altar room to get their shoes. "Wait here."

She dropped Albert's boots on the floor directly in front of him. He was still standing there rubbing his eyes. "Better yet?"

"Getting there." He rubbed both eyes with his knuckles and then blinked repeatedly. “What the hell was that?"

"A release spell, a ward spell, and a luck spell."

"A luck spell, really?"

"It can't hurt."

"I suppose not."

Beverly held the necklace up for Albert to put on again. He reached out and grabbed the charm hard with one hand. He waited a moment and let go. When Jax did not let out a blood curdling scream, he bowed his head and allowed Beverly to slip it on him. "Alright, now what?"

"Now we try to find where they took the statue of Don-gorul. If the stars align Friday night, we are running out of time, and ways, to stop them from releasing him."

"How do you propose we do that?"

"Bait."

"Bait? What do you mean bait?"

"They came after you. They want or need something from you. I don't know what it could be, but they failed. My hope is that they will try again."

"What? No. There is absolutely no reason for them to come after me. I don't have or know anything. I don't think he was after me, specifically. He was in my house, sure, but I don't think he was there to attack me."

"What else would he have been there for? And that's exactly what he did now isn't it?"

"Shit!" Albert was not in the mood for this. He just wanted to go on with his miserable life just the way it was before. He had a feeling things would never be the same again. He wanted the hope though. "I'm tired of all of this bullshit already. Why can't they pick on somebody else? I'm not bait material, I'm just a crazy guy. Why can't they go after somebody else?"

"It's that or we take it to them."

"What do you mean we take it to them?"

We find them and stop their plan in its tracks."

<Oh yeah. You are just gonna go striding into their lair and demand they stop their foolishness. All motherly and what not? That absolutely won't work. They already know Albert. He's a big enough guy, but squishy. They might give him a second glance, but he's not going to get very far either.>

"What do you think we should do then?"

Jax had been thinking about this for a while. If he could convince them that him being free was a good, and helpful idea, he could end up being released. That would mean very good things for him.

CHAPTER 17

"Absolutely not!" Beverly exclaims.

Albert recoils as the sound and tone of her voice booms in his face.

"I can't believe you would even suggest it!"

"Well, technically, I didn't. Jax did. Is it not possible?" Albert put his hands up to defend himself if the question pushed her over the edge.

"Of course, he did, and no, it's not impossible. It's just...complicated, and THE WORST IDEA EVER!" Beverly bowed up in Albert's face again.

"Okay, look. You're a lady, and I know Jax is inside me, but I can't have you bowing up on me like that. I have my limits and you are pushing them being up in my face like this. Yelling at Jax and not me doesn't make it ok."

"You're right. I'm sorry." Beverly turned away and looked at the ground.

"I get that it's not the best idea ever, but I think it's the best idea we've got. It's been a long and trying day. Let's sleep on it. If nothing else comes to us by morning, we can explore it again. Deal?"

Beverly rubbed between her eyes. "Yeah. That sounds like a

good plan. Revisit it in the morning. go on home. I'll close up here and head there myself. Meet back here around 9am?"

"Nine sharp. Right here. Got it. Good night Beverly." Albert showed himself out.

***

Albert climbs into his truck and heads toward the house. He is extremely tempted to pass the house and head straight for the beach. "It's a little too early and it would still be crowded with people. No rest in that." he said out loud to no one.

<Plus, the last place you want to be if the monks attack again is out on a crowded beach.> Jax replies.

Albert heads toward the house. "Tomorrow we will figure things out and sort out how we are going to find the occult of the shadow ninja monks. Tonight, we rest."

Beverly had told him the name of the group, but it hadn't registered with his brain and at the moment, he was too tired to care.

Albert looks in his mirror and sees a long black car that he had seen parked at the gallery. He drove past it as he left. He hadn't given it any thought at the time, but it was now behind him. He was still in the heart of town, so he decided not to panic.

He and Jax had their first calm and collected conversation in a long time. They discussed Jax's past. Albert wanted to know what it was that made Beverly so angry with him, but he avoided asking the question. The last thing he wanted right now was to get Jax all riled up. The quiet conversation was new, and he found he was actually enjoying not being completely alone at the moment.

Jax made jokes about shadow ninja monks and Albert laughed. He told him that it was the best way he could think of to describe them. Jax understood but told Albert that he watches way too much tv. Albert guessed he was right.

When Albert had driven about 20 more minutes, he looked in the mirror and found that the black car was still behind him. He had already passed the point where most traffic turned off and was nearly to the turn off toward his house. He quickly eyeballed the fuel gauge and inhaled. He didn't remember exhaling.

His gut was now screaming at him that this was not simply someone going the same direction as him. There wasn't much out where he lived. He decided rather than sit here and panic, he would test it.

Albert pressed on the accelerator and clenched the steering wheel. He knew this stretch of road well and could get away with almost 80 miles an hour before he would have to slow down for the curve up ahead. He had taken the curve at about 10 miles over the posted speed limit of forty miles an hour, but anything faster than that was asking for trouble.

When the black car didn't shrink off in the distance, he knew. He was being followed. "Shit!" Albert took a deep breath.

<What? What's wrong? You didn't forget to fill up the gas tank, again did you?>

"No, we are good on gas. We aren't going straight home though."

<Why, what's up?>

"We are being followed."

<Followed by what?>

"A car? What else would be following us?"

<I don't know. Could be anything at this point. Disappearing shadow ninja monks?>

"Probably."

<How do you know they are following us?>

"Because I am driving at dangerous speeds and they are keeping up."

<Oh. Well...what are you going to do? There's not exactly anywhere to lose them out here.>

"I know." Albert's thoughts were racing. He knew what was coming up and had to think quickly. He couldn't go home. His gut advised him against it. As long as they kept moving and the car was only following, but that would only last so long. It was nearing dark and soon it would be difficult to see anything out in the middle of nowhere.

<What are you going to do Albert?>

Albert didn't have a plan worked out. He slammed on the breaks. The small pickup skid and dovetailed. He punched the accelerator again and got back up to speed. The car was far enough behind to avoid slamming into the back of him. It backed off but sped up again as soon as he did.

Albert's heart started to race. Sweat was building on his brow. Jax kept up with the questioning. Panic washed through Albert making it difficult for him to think straight.

He slammed on the breaks again and turned the wheel sharply to the right. The trucks wheels skidded and squealed on the pavement as they hugged and made a sharp turn on to Overmine road. Once he was around the corner and the truck was going in the right direction, he floored it again.

Albert chuckled when he checked his mirrors and watched

the black car pass the turn off. It skidded to a stop and backed up. It made the turn behind him and, in a moment flat was on his tail again. There was no doubt he was being followed now. "Shit!"

Albert pressed so hard on the gas that he was certain his foot was going to go through the old rusted floor of his pickup. He needed to find out why they were following him. It had been a day full of disbelief and not know and he had reached his limit on it. He slammed his boot hard on the breaks. The poor old pick up shook and shimmied as it slid to a stop in the middle of the gravel road.

Albert slammed the gearshift into park and jerked the handle on the door. He shoved the door open while he unhooked his seat belt. He reached up under the seat and pulled out a metal pipe. He kept it there for protection, but to date had never needed it. He didn't believe in guns and had never needed one, but now was wishing he had something a little more menacing than an old metal pipe.

He stepped out away from the truck and waited. He knew that as quickly as they had been traveling a collision was likely. He wanted to make sure he was out of the way when it happened. He managed about 4 steps toward the side of the narrow dirt road when he heard sliding on the gravel and the loud crunch of aluminum and fiberglass scraping against steel.

When Albert turned around, it was just in time to see both vehicles meld into one and slide forward about twenty feet. They weren't playing around.

CHAPTER 18

Albert swung the pipe up over his shoulder and took a few steps toward the vehicles. When the back doors and then the front doors opened, he changed his grip on the pipe. He was about to be facing off with at least 4 individuals. He chose a batter's stance, with the pipe at the ready.

He didn't recognize any of the people that stepped out of the vehicle. None of them were bald or wearing black cloaks. In fact, one of them was a woman. He only had a second to think about whether he could actually hit her. When it crossed his mind that if it came down to him or her, he would be the one walking away. He closed his eyes and waited for them to approach.

"What the hell man?! Why did you just stop in the middle of the road like that? You could have killed somebody." The driver of the vehicle yelled as he approached Albert.

Albert opened his eyes, confused by the question. He expected them to come out swinging, not questioning. He dropped the batter's stance but held on to the pipe tightly. Ready to swing at a second's notice. They didn't seem threatening now, but after the day he's had, he wasn't going to take a chance.

Jax is going crazy and freaking out through all of this, adding fuel to the panic fire.

"Why were you following me? What do you want?" Albert growled.

"Following you?" The passenger in the front seat spoke. We missed our turn and only saw it because you took it. We live at that complex down there."

They were not at all what Albert was expecting. Something wasn't right. They were college kids; much younger than the man he had tied up and assaulted earlier and they looked more scared than he was. He wasn't about to drop the pipe until he was sure he was not in danger, though.

He looked at the car and then back at the kids. None of them seemed to be hurt. He had to be sure though. "Are any of you hurt? Is there anyone else in the car?"

The young woman piped up this time. "No, just us. I think we are all okay. Are you okay?" She started walking toward him. The guys all filed in around her. None of them appeared to be holding weapons, but something about them made him very uneasy. Jax isn't helping quell the situation.

He had been so determined to get answers out of them when he stopped but now, he was so unsure. He had never been so unsure of things in his life. This was not how he wanted to spend the rest of his life. He looked at the group of young people approaching him. He had no idea what to expect, but he closed his eyes and sucked in a breath.

The world seemed to shake around him. Suddenly, he saw the young woman take off at a sprint, straight at him. She leapt into the air and nailed him in the face with her knee. Knocking him backward. He quickly righted himself and caught her in the air. He slammed her down on the ground, hard. He looked up again and the driver was quickly approaching him. He lifted the pipe and swung it at the young man's head. He caught him solidly in the jaw. The young man flew back and landed on the ground with a solid thud.

The third and fourth passengers approached him more slowly from each side. He waited for them to charge and then grabbed each of them by their shirts and stepped backward. The momentum of their movement slammed them into each other. The crunching sound of their faces colliding let Albert know that his move had done some damage. He let go of both and watched them both fall to the ground in a heap.

He opened his eyes and the world shook again. Just in time to see the young woman sprinting toward him He ducked to the right as she leapt into the air, her knee aimed right for him. He caught her in the air and slammed her to the ground. He heard her breath escape her. He stared at her for a long moment, waiting for her to get up. She sucked in a long breath and rolled to her side, coughing.

Albert stood up. He didn't want to kill any of them. He hadn't had enough of a glimpse to see how he got out of this yet, but if it meant that he had to, then he guessed he would. The sake of the whole world was riding on it. He didn't have much time to think before the driver was on the attack. Albert readied the pipe and swung it at his knee. The young man's legs knocked cleanly out from under him mid stride. He fell to the ground. Grasping his leg with both hands he fell on his back with his leg in the air. He screamed in agony.

As the last two passengers approached him, he waited. Instead of grabbing their shirts he waited for them to make contact. He grabbed their heads and pulled them into him. When they were tucked neatly under his arms, he fell to the ground. He knew if he didn't really disable them, he would be here fighting longer than he had any desire to.

He let go of the two young men and stood up. He watched for them to get up. When they didn't, he walked over to the woman that was slowly trying to get to her feet. He grabbed her by the hair and yanked her head backward, so she was looking up at him. "Who sent you and why?"

She spit in his face. He was not prepared for that. He wiped the saliva from his face as he shoved her forward and scraped her face in the gravel. He brought her face back up to meet his. "I'll ask again. Who sent you?" He was no longer afraid.

She opened her mouth to speak but her eyes were drawn to movement behind Albert. He turned and planted a solid punch in the middle of the driver. He flew backward and landed with a double thud as his ass and then his head hit the gravel and slid. Albert was done playing around.

He turned his attention back to the young woman. "Where were we? Oh, right. Who sent you?" Albert's nostrils flared and he could feel heat in his face. Fear took over the young woman's face and the name slipped past her lips in a whisper. "Kovach."

"Kovach?" Albert gently slid his fingers out of the young woman's hair and her hands flew up to her face. He stood up and reached over to pick up the pipe. He swung it back over his shoulder. He looked around at the four injured people on the ground. "Kovach?" He looked at each of their faces waiting for a response.

Each one nodded in turn. Albert shook his head. He

stepped over the two passengers and checked their injuries. Both of their noses were bloody and one of them had a split lip, the other had a bruise building on his cheek. Nothing looked serious. He went to the driver and checked his knee. It might need surgery, but he would live. Albert stood up, shook his head, and walked the rest of the way to his truck. He got in, closed the door, and slammed it into reverse. He backed up slightly until the bumper of the black car lifted off his bumper. He pulled forward and waited for the car to drop to the ground. Albert threw the truck into drive and stuck his head out the window. "See if you can get Kovach's insurance to cover the damages. I will talk to him about my claim personally."

He sped off.

CHAPTER 19

Albert finally pulled into his driveway shortly after dark. He threw the truck in park and got out. He stomped around the to the back and examined the damage. There wasn't much. He had to look closely to find a black scratch just above the bumper.

He patted his old reliable truck on the side and strode inside. It wouldn't have made any sense why, but he and Beverly had already deduced that Kovach was involved somehow. This confirmed it but didn't tell him why.

He sat down in his recliner and kicked the feet up. He rubbed his tired eyes and yawned. Feeling like he might be able to relax now, Jax started in.

<You gotta be more careful man! You coulda died out there!>

"You know their intent was to attack me, right? I just beat them to the punch."

<It doesn't matter. You really must be careful Al.>

"Why Jax. You're immortal. Why are you so worried about it?"

<Because I'm immortal dumb ass. That doesn't make you

immortal and I don't want to be stuck out in the middle of nowhere inside a corpse.>

"Wouldn't you just bounce into the next creature that walks by?"

<You really watch too many movies Al. No. I wouldn't just bounce into another living creature. That's a possession and you aren't possessed, and it's not exactly how it works either. I'm bound to you. We share the same space in a different way. >

"So, what would happen?"

<If you die, and Beverly doesn't know where you are, until she finds you or she dies, I'm stuck inside your corpse until well after you become dust.>

"What happens to you when I become dust?" Albert was quite enjoying this part of learning how things really like a little too much he thought. It was interesting to him though, seeing how things really are from a different perspective always intrigued him.

<I'd be bound to your dust. I'd be inside every single fragment of it I'm more concerned with what would happen to you.>

"Well, that sounds better than being sucked back into hell. What do you mean what would happen to me?"

<You have a demon bound to you Al. You would end up in limbo. You would be not be going to heaven or hell. You are no longer welcome in either place.>

"Is Limbo so bad? I'm more of a reincarnation or no life after death at all kind of guy, so not going to a place made of streets of gold or burn forever doesn't seem like such a bad thing."

<You wouldn't be saying that if you've been to Limbo. It's the most terrifying place I've ever been to or experienced. I never want to go there again. The loneliness clings to you like a wet blanket. Time stretches on for ages, and nothingness. I'll take being stuck here any day over that again.> Jax sounds saddened by the thought.

Albert feels bad. "I'm sorry man, I didn't realize you had been there, or how terrible it must be. I should just get some sleep. We are meeting Beverly in the morning and I want to be well rested before dealing with more of that."

<Indeed. Rest well. I'll keep quiet so you can rest. I have some contemplating to do.>

Albert woke up early and called Beverly. She needed to know about that Kovach's involvement is confirmed. They also needed to work out a plan for how to stop the apocalypse. They only had four days left to do it.

He opted not to tell her about the fight on his way home last night until he was face to face with her. For some reason, he was more comfortable talking about the apocalypse and stopping it than he was about discussing a dirty cop with an attitude sending people to attack him over the phone.

He left the house and made it to the gallery without incident. He was relieved when he got there. The business of being followed and fighting in the middle of nowhere was hard on him. He didn't want to go through it again.

When he arrived at the gallery, Beverly was inside at the desk but had not yet turned the sign to open. She met him at the door and unlocked it to let him in. She locked it right back up after. She seemed tense.

"What happened?"

"What do you mean?"

Albert sensed that something had happened with her since they saw each other last, too. He couldn't imagine what, but with the way things have been going, it could be anything.

"I mean, what happened? You are tense and look a little scared."

"Do I? Hmmm. Nothing happened. I did figure out some stuff though. Tell me, what happened that made you believe without a doubt that Kovach is involved."

"Well, I was followed from here last night. Then I was attacked, by a group of college kids. When I beat out of them who had sent them, they all said Kovach."

"Attacked? Again?"

"Yep. The necklace worked again though. I saw it all before it happened. It wasn't quite the same though."

"I really don't think it's the necklace, Albert. It doesn't work that way."

"Whatever it was. I didn't see it when I got attacked by the monk at my house and I didn't have the necklace. Last night, I had the necklace and I closed my eyes and saw what was about to happen, then it did. I'm convinced it's the necklace."

"You shouldn't use it to beat the crap out of people Albert. There is a balance to using magic. You have to be careful with it." Beverly frowned at him.

"It wasn't like that. Like I said, it was different. I saw what happened, but then when it happened, nothing was the same. None of the punches were right and I didn't see how I got away this time. I avoided seriously injuring anyone even though that is not what happened in the vision, but enough to give up the information.

"Oh, so Kovach sent them to mess you up?"

"I don't know what he sent them to do. I made them wreck their car, we talked for a minute, I had the vision, and the fight was on. There were four of them. I doubt they were there to invite me to coffee."

"Alright, so maybe my idea isn't the best one then." Beverly bit her lip and walked to the storage room. Albert followed behind her.

"What idea?"

"That we should join the occult."

Jax chose that moment to chime in. <It's a great idea!> Jax was clever. <You just need the right person for the job.>

CHAPTER 20

"What???" Albert had heard lots of dumb ideas in his lifetime. This was probably the dumbest. "They know who I am and I'm pretty certain they knew who you were before I ever met you. How would that work?"

"Yeah, what does that mean Jax?" Beverly wondered how it was that Jax knew exactly what she was talking about.

<No one has ever seen me.> Now that he was able to be in the same conversation with the witch, he had a way to escape being shoved into that damned necklace. He had to try.

Beverly thought quietly for a long while. Albert asked a bunch of questions about how that would even work. Jax was inside Albert, how would he be able to get into the occult without being recognized? Could Jax manipulate his look? He didn't know if he was ok with that.

Beverly started to babble something about casting the right kind of spell could do it. She would have to account for several things, like how to get him out, how much energy it would take, where she could get it from without blowing out the entire neighborhood.

Albert couldn't believe what he was hearing. He hadn't seen Beverly do anything more than make a couple of candles spark and a necklace glow. He wasn't convinced that she could remove the voice and make it into an actual being. This was crazy.

"This is crazy!!! You want to take him out of me and make him real? You want to set him free on the world at large with a physical presence? How would you even do that?"

"Do what?"

"Get him out of me?"

Beverly thought long and hard about her answer. It was easily possible. The problem was the consequences of doing so. While the end of the world was clearly at stake, releasing a demon she had imprisoned would be setting a precedent, and not a good one. She would have to think about this.

This particular demon was not all evil. He had done some things that warranted locking him away, but he was not inherently evil. He was contained. Releasing him, even temporarily, could spell disaster on a worldwide scale. Not to mention it could cost her a high position among her people. She had worked very hard to earn her place. She had to tread carefully here.

"I... I could. It could be disastrous though. I don't know that it's the best idea, but it is an idea."

<What could it harm? I go in, get the info we seek, and come out.>

Albert laughed out loud. "You have been tucked away for quite some time now Jax. It's not as easy as walking out. I'm pretty sure they would have firepower, guns and plenty of ammunition, not to mention the brainwashing. You would probably have to go through weeks of orientation and brain washing before they would tell you anything about what they are planning."

Beverly, listening to the discussion between Jax and Albert makes a verbal note that she would have to account for and create an escape. She would have to create a way to get Jax out, in a hurry. She ran to the altar room and came back with an old tome in her hands. She started flipping through pages.

"Do we even know how to find them?" Albert asked.

"I have an idea of where to look. You said you were attacked by college kids?"

"Yes, they said that they lived at a complex out at old Ivermine road."

"How long have you lived here Albert?"

"My whole life."

"What will you find at the end, or anywhere along Ivermine Road?"

"Not much. The old mine is way down at the end...ohhhh. I see."

"Now, I can probably craft a number of spells and make them work together to accomplish what we want, but..." Her voice trailed off and she talked and flipped through pages in the tome again.

"But what?"

<Yeah, but what?>

"We are talking about letting a demon out of its prison. He has committed crimes against humanity and there are rules. I could be throwing away my entire career, and possibly my life if he messes up. Not to mention the chaos he could wreak being unleashed on the world. It's just not a good idea."

Albert thought about that for a long moment. In all their

years together, the only thing terrible he had ever seen Jax do was distract him when he should have been paying attention. He couldn't imagine what kind of trouble he could cause outside of himself. "I have never seen him do anything terrible. What's the worst that could happen?"

"How long did he wait to inform you that he was not just a voice in your head Albert? You can't tell me he hasn't been at all damaging to your life."

Albert got quiet. She made a valid point. He had been the cause, even if indirectly, a lot of horrible things in his life. The loss of his parents, Seralie and Angela. He barely escaped being imprisoned on so many occasions because Jax was constantly getting him into situations that were legally questionable. He didn't know what Jax had done before, but in the past 30 years, being annoying was the worst of his crimes. He thought that had to count for something.

"I just don't think that he would do anything to jeopardize other people's lives. He's always been more concerned with helping people find things that meant a lot to them. Doesn't that count for something?"

"He's a demon Albert." She couldn't shake the turmoil and chaos that he caused in her life. She couldn't look past it. He'd caused her a lot of pain. Losing Jacob was just the beginning. Her people were livid, and she was still working on paying off the debt for everything that was destroyed when she was hell bent on catching Jax.

"What other choice do we have? We are 4 days from the end of the world and have no clue where it's even going to start. If I understand things correctly, if we don't do something, none of it will matter after that anyway."

Beverly had to agree with Albert's logic. She still had a very uneasy feeling about it.

CHAPTER 21

Jax really did want to be free of his prison. To be able to walk freely again would be just what he needed. He would be able to give this bitch what she deserves. Stopping the end of the world had to come first though. <I'll promise to do whatever it takes to help stop the end of the world before I wreak any kind of havoc, if it helps.>

Beverly rolled her eyes. She knew that Jax just being loose to move about the world would wreak havoc. He couldn't help it. It was the nature of the demon. He was trying though. It counted for something.

"Fine. Come on Albert." Beverly turned toward the altar room and strode toward it.

Albert followed. His nerves suddenly caught up with him and he wondered if the process was going to be painful. He had seen exorcisms before, and they looked horrible. He hoped it would be easier if the demon was willing to leave. He couldn't wait to find out. "Wait. Will this hurt?"

Beverly didn't give any indication one way or the other. She strode into the altar room and kicked off her shoes. She padded toward the altar and knelt in front of it as she had before. She turned and nodded at Albert as he was kicking off his boots. He stepped to the center of the gold weave circle, as he had before.

Beverly pulled out the wooden box and shuffled through it. She turned to Albert. "You might want to sit down. Just make sure that all of you is inside the circle. This could take a while."

Albert nodded and sat down. He crossed his legs Indian style and looked all around himself to make sure he was completely inside the circle.

Beverly stood up and walked to where Albert sat. "I need the necklace." Albert clutched it tight in his hand and rubbed his thumb over the smooth dark surface of the stone. He felt much more confident with it. "You don't want to be holding it when he comes into it. Trust me."

Albert thought about it for a moment. Picturing a grotesque being suddenly being in his arms. He nodded and pulled the necklace up over his head and held it out for her. "Are you sure about this?"

"Sure, about what?"

"About this exorcism. I don't see any priests, a bible, or any holy water." Albert smirked.

"You watch too many movies Albert. If this were an exorcism it would be a lot simpler and less risky. It's not though, you should be fine."

That didn't calm Albert's nerves any. "If not an exorcism, then what?"

"I am going to summon him to stand before you inside the circle. He will put on the necklace and I will cast a temporary binding spell, binding him to the necklace. He will have a physical form, but he will not be able to remove the necklace. He goes where it goes. No ifs, ands, or buts."

<Bound to the necklace, but not inside it?>

"Not yet." Beverly bore a devilish grin.

Jax thought about that for a moment. He wasn't happy about it, but it would have to do. He would be happier to be free of the damn necklace, and her. He was terrified of the way things could go if he didn't do this though.

<OK, got it. Thank you. I know the risk and I won't let you down.>

With that, Beverly set the necklace down in the center of the stone tablet again. As she whispered her chant and sprinkled ingredients over the cauldron, the glow around the necklace began to change colors again. Albert sat inside the circle and waited. "Is this going to hurt?"

"I don't know. Never done this before. I'm essentially going to rip a soul out of your body, so it could. Brace yourself."

Every muscle in Albert's body tensed. "Exorcisms always look like they hurt in the movies."

Beverly turned and looked at Albert. "They can and often do, but this isn't an exorcism. It's a temporary extraction. So maybe it won't be as painful as that." She winked.

She turned back to the necklace and started chanting again. Albert, nervous, asked another question, then another, and when he was about to ask a third, Beverly turned and glared at him. She sucked in a breath and exhaled before she spoke.

"I need to concentrate. This must be done exactly right. One false chant or the wrong ingredient and you could end up on Pluto stuck with him forever."

Albert cringed at the thought. Pluto, with Jax sounded far

from appealing. He mimicked turning a key in a lock on his lips and put the key in his pocket. He watched Beverly with his lips sealed.

After a moment or two, Albert started to feel a change. It wasn't pain, it was a giddiness. The thought crossed his mind that maybe he was finally going to be free of the voices in his head.

After a long moment though, he realized that the giddiness was not just his. Jax was excited too. He could feel Jax's movements inside him again. It was a strange feeling.

He held out his hands and looked at them. His eyes widened as he watched each of them turned into two. His and a very transparent second set. He waved them about in front of him. Watching with awe as they trailed his own.

Beverly turned around and looked at Albert. Her eyes opened to three times their normal radius. "It's working." She continued to chant and watched as Albert's form slowly and faintly turned into two.

Her amazement waned as the form of Jax slowly made its way into existence. He was taking shape. A very translucent shape, but a shape. She started to chant louder. He would need more than a ghostly appearance. She chanted louder and louder. Forgetting that he was a powerful deity, she wondered for a moment if she would have the power that she needed to bring him forth.

She chanted louder and his form became more and more opaque but slowly. She was going to need more. She chanted louder and louder.

A wind started to blow from nowhere inside the small space. The flames of the candles flickered and rocked from side to side on their wicks. The light bouncing and dancing around along the curtain walls was almost dizzying. Jax's form started to fill in. He was still very easy to see through, but it seemed to be working.

CHAPTER 22

Beverly stopped chanting. She looked around the room and spoke to Jax. "Now is the time to choose your appearance Jaxolox. Picture what you want to look like and concentrate on it."

Albert and Beverly watched the still ghostly form change before their eyes. The finger nails lengthened and turned a deep red. The fingers themselves elongated and grew slender. The color of the skin paled and smoothed.

"Jax! Be serious. Do you really want to be a woman for this?" Albert shouted.

Beverly cackled. "Probably the best thing he could be." She went back to chanting.

The form continued to change. The finger nails receded and grew white. The fingers remained long but plumped up like hot dogs cooking on a grill. The skin hardened and stretched over muscle that wasn't there a moment before. Large veins appeared, slightly raised under the skin. The tone darkened to an olive brown.

The still fair image of a third person in the room slowly started to rise and forward, away from Albert. He unfolded and stood, still inside the circle. Beverly nodded and turned back toward the altar, focusing her attention on the necklace now. She dropped more ingredients into the cauldron and a few over the necklace itself.

The tapered candles on either side of the tablet sparked and whizzed with electricity shooting between them. The flames were large and bright, and a blue-white line of energy flowed between them and to the necklace. The glow around the necklace changed colors at a rapid pace and grew brighter.

Beverly picked up the necklace and turned back toward Albert and Jax in the center of the room. She was taken aback when she saw the form Jax had chosen. A tall, dark haired man was in front of Albert, still seated on the floor. He floated in the air. Arms at his sides, he slowly looked up to meet Beverly's stare.

She noticed that his eyes were dark and menacing. Something about them made her skin feel warm and cold at the same time. She broke the stare and looked down. She gazed over the brazenly male shape he had chosen to take, floating there in front of her, naked.

Jax followed her gaze and raised an eyebrow as he watched her facial expression change and color filled her cheeks. <Not too shabby, huh?> He turned with his arms out, allowing her a view of the rest of him as well.

Beverly rolled her eyes. "Ugh, I think it worked." She didn't bother looking over the rest of him. She turned and picked up the necklace and turned back toward Jax. She continued to chant loudly as she approached him. His form taking a more solid appearance than even a moment ago.

"Hey! Turn around. You nearly put my eye out asshole!"

Beverly laughed out loud as she stepped forward. She

motioned for Albert to stand up. When he was on his feet, she motioned him out of the center circle. Albert took 2 large steps backward. He continued to stare in awe of what was happening.

Jax continued to float in the air between them. The necklace still glowing a dark green, she lifted it in the air and chanted something new, again in a language that Albert had never heard before.

She kept the necklace held up right and looked at Jax. Repeat after me Jax. "Nobu sobe kulu tut."

<Nobut sobe kulu tut?> Jax repeated what he thought he heard.

Beverly nodded and spoke it again. Louder than the first time and enunciated the tone.

Jax matched the volume and repeated the words again. <Nobu sobe kulu tut. Nobu sobe kulu tut.>

As they spoke, the necklace's green glow morphed into a solid white and she started to lower it over Jax's head.

Albert recalled the blindness that overtook him earlier and instinctively closed and shielded his eyes with his arm. The necklace grew brighter and brighter as they chanted.

"It's not bright enough. Albert, repeat after me. Nobu sobe kulu tut."

Albert whispered what he thought he heard. "New boo so be Cthulhu tut?"

"No time for jokes Albert, repeat the words exactly like I do, or the spell won't work." She slowed the chant down. "Nobu sobe."

"Nobu sobe." Albert repeated her exactly.

"Kulu tut."

"Kulu tut? That doesn't make any sense."

"Doesn't matter. Just say it."

"Fine. Nobu sobe kulu tut."

Beverly rolled her eyes. "Look. Say it right or you will turn into a toad. Words matter. Tone matters. Rhythm matters. Nobu sobe kulu tut."

Albert tucked away his humor for the moment. He didn't know if magic worked that way, but he didn't want to find out by ending up being a toad. "Nobu sobe kulu tut."

Beverly smiled and nodded.

As he chanted out the right words the right way, he watched the necklace start to glow brighter. As he grew confident with the words, he spoke them louder and louder, and each time with more conviction than the last. He made a note to himself to ask Beverly what it was that he had said later.

Beverly continued to chant and encouraged the other to as well until the necklace reached a super brightness that her eyes couldn't take. She dropped the necklace and shielded her eyes.

As the chain settled on Jax's shoulders and the charm slapped gently against Jax's now solid chest, an ear-piercing crack and a ripple of light flowed out in all directions. The force of the sound threw Beverly and Albert backward.

The curtains that enclosed the small dark space flew open with gale force winds. The solid walls of the storage room shook and rattled around them. The bright fluorescent bulbs in the light fixtures above them shattered. Darkness and glass fell around them.

CHAPTER 23

Albert stood up and looked around. It was dark in the room, but there, in the middle of the rug, stood Jax, in all his naked glory, staring down at the charm that hung on a chain like a heavy weight. The glow emanating from the necklace was the only light in the room and it was faint.

He looked beyond Jax to where Beverly had been standing and found a pile of rubble that used to be her beautiful altar. She was a mangled mess of curtains with bright red hair. She wasn't moving.

Albert rushed past Jax and flew to Beverly's side. He knelt beside her and blew and patted out the flames of the candles that threatened to set the room on fire. He brushed away the debris of broken glass and wood and fumbled with the swath of velvet black that wrapped around her.

She whimpered. She was hurt. He didn't know how badly, but guessing from the amount of debris around her, he hoped not as bad as it looked. He helped her sit up. She winced and held her left arm at a weird angle. "Are you hurt?" He asked.

"Just my arm. I'll be ok. What happened?"

"I don't know. The necklace started to glow, and we got thrown away from it. Are you sure you are ok?"

"Yeah, I'm fine. This will heal in a few minutes and I'll be good as new. Where's Jax?"

"Still standing there in the middle of the room. This didn't affect him at all it doesn't seem." He looked over at Jax's new physical form.

Jax stood there, almost stone still. He didn't appear to be breathing. Just standing, his head tilted forward, his shoulders sunken and a look of despair covered his face.

Albert gave Beverly a questioning look and looked back at Jax. "He is fine. Probably a little sad, maybe a little disgusted, but he is fine."

"Sad? Disgusted? Why would he be either of those things? He is free."

"No. No, he isn't. He is bound."

"He has a human body. He can move about the world now. How is that not free?"

"Silly human. Human form is not freedom. It is for you humans. You can move about and think that you are free. He is a demon. He has had at least a thousand years, free to move about any realm he chose. This is not freedom for him."

"Here we go with this kind of talk again. Why do you speak like you know something about it?"

"I'm more like him than I am like you." She released her arm and started to rub around it gently. She chanted quietly. As she did, she straightened and twisted her arm. Albert heard popping and cracking sounds. The obviously broken arm under the long sleeve was repairing itself. It kind of grossed him out.

Albert stood and watched, again in awe and confusion. He didn't think he would understand how all of this worked. He was quite certain he didn't want to. He hoped that at some point he would wake up and find it had all been a dream. "I can't believe this."

<Believe it. It's happening. I hope it is worth it. We must find this occult and stop them. Why are we standing around?>

Jax lifted his head. He would have to make the best of this and figure out how to fix it later. Right now, they needed to move on with their plan. He didn't want to stay like this any longer than he had to.

Albert helped Beverly to her feet. Her arm was almost completely repaired, and she was steady on her feet. He looked at her and then at Jax. She nodded. Albert walked slowly to Jax.

"Are you alright?"

<I'm, ok. This feels...weird...and squishy. I don't know how you can stand to live like this.>

Albert looked at Jax's new form. From he where he was standing, Jax looked anything but squishy. He was solid. He was built like Hercules and was gorgeous as men go. "What do you mean 'like this'?"

<I suppose you wouldn't know the difference. It doesn't matter. It will be over with soon. Let's go so I can get out of here.>

Beverly approached him. She looked him over again. "We need to find you something to wear. You can't exactly go out into the world like this. You look a little...cold." She jabbed at Jax's ego. "I think I know exactly what you need."

Jax reeled as the words landed in his ears. He glared at Beverly. He didn't find her criticism of his chosen body parts humorous. From the inside, he probably wouldn't have cared at all. Being on the outside, though, made him feel vulnerable and weak. He didn't like it. <You will not speak so unkindly of it when you are impaled with it.>

Albert's head snapped. He could not believe the words that had just spilled out of his voice's mouth. He puffed up and jumped between Jax and Beverly. Breaking Jax's glare at Beverly he challenged the god standing before him now.

"You will not speak of doing that, or anything like it, ever again. This is not how we humans behave, and you will not give us a bad name. Do you hear me, Jax?"

Albert had never been powerful or scary. He meant what he said though and he would have none of it. He would not allow Jax, something that he still considered a part of himself to behave so crudely.

Jax was un-deterred. He didn't have any reason to be kind to the witch that imprisoned him, twice now. He would not be kind. He would damage her in any and every way that he could, when he had the ability.

His anger flowed in his words. <I'll not be kind to the witch that trapped me and has now convinced me that it is a good idea to be here. She will die at my hand, even if the world doesn't end.>

Albert took a step backward. He didn't know this man. He assumed that he would be the same as the voice that was in his head all this time. He was now, for the first time, seeing what it was that Beverly had been talking about. He had a feeling, now, that she might have been right to do what she did to him.

CHAPTER 24

Beverly was not afraid. She knew that he was powerful, among the ranks of his kind. She also knew that he was clever and devious. He would do anything he possibly could to escape her. She knew it, and she planned accordingly with her spells.

"I believe it worked, but we should still test it. Tell me you understand your job Jaxolox."

<Aye. I know what I need to do.>

"Explain it then."

Jax shot a cutting glare at Beverly. <I told you that I know what I am to do. Why do you question me still?>

"Because I demand it, and you will obey." She proudly and confidently stepped up to meet the demon eye to eye. "I called you, and you will do, and only do, what I have summoned you to do. Do you understand?"

A low grumble started inside Jax. It grew louder and more like a growl. He lifted his arm as if he was going to strike Beverly down. He built tension in the muscles and joints until his arm was shaking. He threw the punch.

As his shoulder released the tension and it slung forward toward Beverly, Albert reacted. He started to move toward

Beverly and shield her from the blow. She put her hand up to stop him. She stood there, solid and unafraid, waiting.

A bright light flashed in the room. Jax squealed and whelped like an injured dog. The sound echoed through the large room. Jax cradled his hand and blew out the flames that had engulfed it.

Albert stood back and laughed. A roar poured from his deepest regions and echoed through the room. He didn't know why he thought this funny, but he did. "Ok you two. Put your penises away and let’s get on with this. We are running out of time.

Beverly nodded. "You are right. Let's get on with this. Do you want to drive or shall I?"

"You have a bigger vehicle. All 3 of us won't fit in my truck. So, I suppose, you."

"Alright. A word of advice, before we leave here. Do not trust him. He is not your friend. He is not concerned with anything but himself right now. It was different when he had your conscience to filter him. Now he does not. He will deceive you. Be prepared."

"Okay, you're scaring me. Stop that. Wait here. I might have some extra clothes in my truck." Albert turned and stomped out of the room. On his way I he started to turn around. He thought about how Jax's hand caught on fire as he swung a punch at Beverly. He laughed again, realizing that they would be just fine. He picked up his shoulders and half-skipped out to his truck.

When he returned, he was shocked. There was rubble and debris everywhere. Jax and Beverly were nowhere to be found. There were small flames burning all around the back of the room. He knew there had been a lot of damage and debris in the room, but now it seemed like there was even more.

The lights had been blown out throughout the room, but there were small fires burning in places around the room. The flames gave a cozy, almost romantic effect. The altar room that had once stood in the corner was now a pile of writhing and wiggling black velvet.

Albert rolled his eyes. "Are you fucking serious? Is this how it is going to be? The end of the world is coming, and you guys are teenagers that can't control your hormones!" He stomped over toward the edge of the sea of velvet and yanked.

There they were, wrapped up together, writhing and moaning. Completely ignoring Albert's presence. He dropped the curtain, let the clothes he had carried in under his arm fall to the floor with a swoosh, and clomped out of the room.

CHAPTER 25

Albert stormed into the gallery. He had some time to kill and calm down. He couldn't be too angry. Jax, if he understood things correctly, was a demon and had demon needs. One of which, he assumed, was a sexual one. Albert imagined that if he had been forced to go if Jax had without it, he would probably take advantage of the situation too. He just hoped that he hadn't done it the way he talked about it. From the looks of things, there was a bit of a heated discussion about it before hand, but the final act was consensual based on Beverly's moans. He would just have to look the other way.

He killed time walking around the gallery. He found he now had a whole new appreciation for the artwork it contained. If what he had been told was correct, this was a prison. A fancy and contemporary decorated one, but still a prison. He looked deeply into the paintings. Nothing seemed extraordinary or particularly beautiful, but they peaked his imagination. He stood staring at one painting, scratching his chin. He imagined what it was like, being trapped inside this painting. Jax came out of the storage room. Dressed and reeking of sweat and shame. He nodded at Albert.

Beverly came out of the room behind him, hopping on

one foot as she tried to make egress and put on a heel at the same time. Albert laughed out loud. He usually had a good deal of couth about this kind of thing, but seeing her hop on one foot, hair all disheveled, clothes out of place, and her face a shade of crimson he had never seen on a human before, he just couldn't help it. Laughter bounced off the white plaster walls of the gallery.

Beverly flipped him the bird, slammed her lifted foot to the floor and took two steps to keep herself from falling over. "There was a reason he was imprisoned."

Jax turned and looked at Albert, then at Beverly, then back to Albert again. "No shame in it. I have needs and I know how to meet them."

"Did you at least remember to put the fires out? You weren't in there long."

"Shit!" Beverly turned and stormed back into the room.

Jax and Albert bellowed with laughter together. They followed her into the room and helped her douse the flames around the room. Albert tried to wrap his head around the scene. Knowing that Jax would catch on fire any time he tried to harm Beverly, and gauging by the placement of all the little fires around the room, there was a chase for sure.

Beverly stood in the corner, just a foot away from the pile of black velvet she had been engulfed in a few moments before. She turned and looked around the room. She shook her head, in disgust, before straightening herself, raising her hands, and chanting.

The flames around the room dwindled and went out at the same time. Albert's jaw hit the floor. He rushed in to help her douse the flames and had grabbed the first piece of fabric he could find and was running for the first fire to his left. He had a beautifully intricate tapestry bunched up in a ball over his head, ready to toss and stomp on. When the fires were all out, Beverly rushed over to him. She yanked the tapestry away from him. "Don't ever try to use anything in here to put out a fire. You have no idea what you could have done." She scolded him.

"I'm sorry. Stuff was on fire. What was I supposed to do?"

"Work some magic, call the fire department, but never use an item from here to put out a fire."

"Why, what's the worst that would have happened?" Albert wasn't trying to be a dick, he really didn't understand why she was upset at him for trying to help.

"With that tapestry, we would have double the trouble on our hands. The demon Aziriel is trapped in that one."

Jax let out a long slow whistle. "That would have been bad. Dongorul is going to be hard enough to defeat if he gets out. Aziriel too? No way in hell we are getting out of that alive."

Beverly nodded. "Fire is the only thing that can break my spells, because they are created with fire."

"The whole room was on fire!" Albert yelled. Confused and frustrated by the new knowledge. "Why is it that by trying to save the room, I'm wrong, but you two set it on fire and it's ok? This is bullshit!" Albert stormed out of the room.

"He's got a lot to learn. You are horrible for shielding him from all of this. He should have learned the rules a long time ago."

"How was I supposed to know that he would need to know this stuff one day?"Jax asked and shrugged.

Beverly punched him in the arm as she blazed past him

after Albert. "You are a demon, you know. You know it always comes to needing to know."

Jax hung his head. "I know. I just hoped it never would."

"Well now look what you have done!"

Jax accepted the scolding. He did know, and he did hope that he would never have to deal with this kind of thing. He really should have thought better and told Albert, at least a little. Now, it's just a shock to him and he is fighting against it. That had the potential to get them all killed now. Albert needed to know. He turned and walked out of the room.

"We really need to go." Beverly said as she approached the glass desk and picked up her keys and purse. She didn't want to dwell on what was past. They were running out of time and they needed to get Jax to the compound. They needed his intelligence. She laughed at the thought and sighed.

CHAPTER 26

Jax inhales a deep breath and exhales it slowly. He opens the car door. He has never been nervous before. He's never been under this kind of pressure before either though. He knows the strength and destruction that Dongorul can deliver. The last thing he wants is to be responsible for the end of the world. He stands up, adjusts his clothes, and strides toward the mine. He has no idea what he is going to do, but whatever it takes, he must get inside.

He is met by a hand full of men in cloaks. Their heads are bald, and they form a line at the gate. The one in the middle steps forward. He extends his hand and says something welcoming in an occult-y way. Jax tries to contain his laughter. The idea of a deep loyalty such as this never fails to astonish him. He needs to get inside though, so he must play along. He smiles and nods. He hopes to god that the head shaving is a privilege he must work up to.

He explains who he is, a made-up story of course, and why he is there.

"I'm Nicholas. I'm on the run and need some help. I've gotten caught up in the middle of some terrible stuff that had nothing to do with me and need somewhere to gather my thoughts and figure out what to do. The folks around town told me this might be a place I could do that. God's not much been on my side of late, so maybe you guys know an alternative that would be?"

A simultaneous "aww" comes from the line of monks along the fence. "Blessings be upon you by the Lady Sophia. The monk standing in front of Jax nods and holds out his hand.

Jax turns and nods at the vehicle he stepped out of and it pulls away. Jax is now at the mercy of this group of hooded fools.

He knows he is short on time. The last thing he wants to do is take months trying to work his way up through the ranks. He needs to meet the highest member of the gathering, and quick. It's already mid-morning on Thursday. He takes the hand offered to him and gives it a hearty shake. When he lets go, the monk in front of him turns to the others and the line that blocked him before is now parted.

Jax takes a deep breath and steps forward. The monk beside him walks beside him. The monk begins to ask him questions. Jax, with his obnoxious manner makes a joke about monks and vows of silence. The monk gives him a scolding look. Jax expresses repentance for his behavior. It's a habit and it's his first day. The monk nods and they continue walking.

Jax is taken to a room. In it, there is a pair of clippers on a mirrored table, a cloak hanging on a hook next to the table, and a twin-size bed. The room itself a good size, but cold and damp. He figured they were about 30 feet underground and this must have been either a storage area or a bad vein at one point in time. He turned and looked at the monk. The monk smiled, nodded, and turned to go. Jax made a comment about no reading material being present. The monk laughed. He pointed at the drawer on the front of the table and laughed. Jax looked where he pointed, smacked himself in the head, and laughed with him. The monk closed the door as he left.

Jax turned in a full circle and looked around the room. He hadn't heard the lock click on the door. He assumed that it had though. He didn't want to try it right away. He needed to know how these people worked. The only way to do that was to find the reading material and browse it. He strode to the mirrored table and opened the drawer. There was reading material alright. A small black bound book with a ribbon coming out of it. Brightly colored tri-fold brochures were stacked next to it, beside that was a pen case with the symbol that the monks had on their hoods emblazoned on the front of it. Beside that was a stapled together paper packet.

Jax pulled the paper out and flipped through it. It was all blank. He put it back and pulled out a brochure. He read the front, and then flipped it open. There he found some of the information he was looking for. Their leader, who chose to be called Josiah, welcomes you. Jax laughed out loud. The guy looked like a tv evangelist. He wasn't wearing a cloaked hood, or anything fancy. A light blue button-down shirt, with a white t-shirt underneath.

He asked questions through the brochure like have you had a rough life, are you looking for somewhere to turn that will forgive your past and only look toward your future. Jax hadn't had a rough life, not from his sense of it. He didn't give a rat's ass what his future looked like or how anyone else felt about it. He was a demon. These types of things were human things. He had no use for them. He felt sad when the thought about the humans that did though. Humans like Albert. Albert could easily be swayed by a brochure and questions like this.

He put the brochure back and picked up the small book. It looked like a bible. The little gold ribbon hanging out the bottom appeared to be flipped over the page right in the middle. He shrugged and decided to start there. He opened the book right in the middle and started reading. He stifled a laugh. The first passage read of how forgiveness was a gift for a chosen few. When one knew they were chosen, they would find themselves here, reading this passage. This was the start of their journey to a greater future. He read down a little and turned the page. There were no scriptures, like a bible, just page after page of psychobabble. He turned to the last page.

There it was. The passage that told him to shave his head, don the cloak, and start his journey today. It also said that if now was not the right time, that was ok. He could leave whenever he chose. His gut told him this would be the moment to do just that. Nothing seemed right about this. Maybe it was because he knew what was in store for the people that bought in to this, but any smart thinking man should be able to see through it. Now he was curious. He wasn't about to shave his head and wear a cloak, but he was curious. What could this guy possibly say that would convince a man to shave his head? He took the book and walked over to the bed.

He plopped back on the hard pillow and kicked up his feet. He turned to the first page in the book and began reading. Time didn't seem to matter now. He read the first page and turned to the second one. "This guy is good." He exclaimed to himself. If he makes it out of this, I might just make him follow me and recruit people to worsh..." There was a knock at the door.

Jax sat upright as the door opened and a new monk, a young kid probably no older than twenty, stepped through the door. He stepped into the room never looking up from the floor. "Josiah wishes to see you." Jax dropped the book on the bed and took three strides toward the young man. Jax looked him over. It broke his heart. This kid, barely old enough to know the joys of yanking his own chain, was here, in a hood with a bald head, giving up everything, to be swallowed by a world devouring demon. He kept his thoughts to himself but felt very bad for this young one in the prime of his life. "Well let's go then." Jax waited for the monk to turn toward the door so he could follow him.

The monk stood there and finally lifted his head. He looked at Jax and then at the cloak hanging on the wall. Jax followed his gaze. "Oh, right." Jax grabbed the cloak and slipped it on as he strode out the door. He wasn't about to shave his head if he didn't have to. The young monk shrugged and caught up with Jax.

CHAPTER 27

Albert is apprehensive as they drive away. Leaving Jax standing in front of a crowd of people dressed just like the guys that have attacked him twice now.

"He'll be fine Albert. Remember, he's immortal. The worst they can do to them is imprison him in something. It shouldn't take even if they tried because he's already bound."

"If you say so. I still feel kinda bad leaving the poor guy there with them his first day as a human. It's like dropping a baby off in a lion's den and hoping they don't eat it."

Beverly laughed out loud. "It's more the opposite. We just dropped a lion off in a playroom full of children. He'll be fine. You hungry? I'm starving."

Albert looked over his shoulder one more time. Jax was being escorted in the gate and the crowd of bald heads gathered behind him. Albert sighed.

"Yeah. I could eat. What are you in the mood for?"

"I know this great little diner out on 84."

"Jim's Diner?"

"Yeah. You know it?"

"Oh yea. Great little place. Jim was a friend of my dad's.

We ate there a lot when I was growing up. I haven't been there in a while. Be nice to be back there maybe. Let's go."

They rode the rest of the way to the diner in silence.

Albert and Beverly went inside and took a seat. Albert looked around and noticed the place hadn't changed too much. There was a new flashy jukebox in the corner and the product pictures were different, but otherwise it looked just like he remembered it.

The waitress, a dainty blonde in form fitting black pants and a button down white with green stripes approached. "Hey folks. Welcome to Jim's Diner. What can I get you to drink?" She asked as she set silverware and glasses of water down in front of them.

Albert ordered coffee and Beverly ordered a sweet tea. "Is Jim around? He's an old friend of the family and I'd like to say hello." Albert asked the waitress.

"Sure is sugar. I'll send him right on over." She turned and sauntered off to get their drinks.

"Friendly girl that one." Albert said to Beverly. An attempt to break the awkward silence that had developed between them.

"Yeah. That's Jesse. She used to be a man. Been working here about seven years now. Just as awesome after the change as before."

Albert turned and looked at her over his shoulder. She was talking to a man about his age at the drink station. "I never would have guessed. Wait, Jim's youngest son Jesse?"

"One and the same."

"Wow." The man Jesse was talking to a moment before approached with their drinks and set them on the table in front of them. "A little bird tells me you fine folks asked to speak with me?"

Albert looked up and eyed the man. "Jimmy? Jimmy Dickson?"

"Yeah, that's right. Who might you be and what can I do for you?"

"Holy shit man. You got old. I was expecting your dad. You don't remember me, do you?"

"Can't say that I do. I don't remember much these days though. Picked myself up a brain tumor and it plays with my memory."

"Man, I'm sorry to hear that. I'm Albert. My parents, Rose and Alfred, and I used to come in here a lot. You and I, and little Jesse over there used to run around these tables together."

"Oh my. I vaguely remember that! They were in the accident in..."

"Ninety-seven. Yeah, that's them."

"So, how have you been. It's been a while."

They make small talk and catch up, avoiding the topic of the pending end of the world as Beverly sits quietly sipping her sweet tea.

"Pardon my manors." Albert glances at Beverly. "This is an associate and friend of mine Beverly, this is Jimmy. Jim, the owner's son."

"I'm actually the owner now. Dad passed away a few years ago and I took over the place." Jimmy interjected as he reached his hand out to Beverly.

"I'm so sorry to hear that. I'm glad it's you that took it

over. It just wouldn't be the same feel belonging to someone else." Beverly replied.

"Thanks. So, what else can I get you?" Jimmy asked.

Albert was dumbfounded and feeling guilty. He spent a lot of time with these people when he was younger, their father passed away a few years ago and he had no idea. He really needed to be better about keeping in touch.

They placed their order with Jimmy, and he went to make it. Albert looked at Beverly silent and brooding for a long moment. Finally, he spoke. "You knew the family as well, then?"

"Somewhat. We didn't spend time together outside of the diner here, but I come here a lot."

Albert nodded his head. This family, and many more like them being destroyed by Dongorul flashed through his mind. He looked around the diner. "So, what do I need to know about this Dongorul. How do we stop him? More importantly, how are we going to know when Jax has the information we need. We didn't exactly arrange a pick-up time."

"We'll know. As for Dongorul, if we get there in time to stop the ritual, nothing. We just must yank the statue and prevent the ritual from being carried out. If he does get out, then I'll just need to trap him in something else. It's really all we can do with demons. Just, if he does get set free, don't get in his way. Defend me while I do the ritual to put him back."

Albert cringed less at the word now. It doesn't all make sense to him, but with what all he has seen now, it's starting to come together. Beverly spoke of it so matter of factly. Like it was common place for her. "So, it's stopped the ritual or...?"

"Or, he starts destroying everything around him. Eating everyone and everything in his path."

"Ok. Movie reference time. Are we talking Godzilla or Cthulhu here?"

Beverly rolled her eyes. "Yes. Dongorul is what you get if you breed Godzilla and Cthulhu together. The destruction he will cause in a short amount of time will be devastating. He will destroy the mine in moments. If he gets out of there, the rest of the world in a matter of days."

"Holy shit!" Albert rubs his face with his hands.

"Yeah."

They finished their lunch and Beverly dropped Albert back off at the gallery.

"Go home and get some rest. I'll call you as soon as I know anything." Beverly said as she parked and headed into the gallery.

Albert nodded and headed for his truck. He made it home without incident. He didn't make it much further though.

CHAPTER 28

He led Jax down the long corridor, through pathways that were dimly lit. There were forks and turns and all manner of places a person could get lost. Lucky for Jax, he wasn't a person. He would be able to find his way back to his room, and the exit, easy peasy. They finally came upon a large opening. It was brightly lit with thousands of candles. It was a large open space with a stage that looked like it had been cut into the wall. In the center of it was a large painted portrait of Josiah, arms out stretched and smiling at his flock.

Jax assumed this was where they gathered, probably several times a day, to hear a lesson from Josiah and worship him. That thought gave him the chills. There was no amount of babble from this man that Jax wanted littering his ears. He also noticed, that below the painting, in the middle of this massive stage, was a tiny statue. More like a statuette. A naked woman that looked like it had been carved out of ivory. It was long and slender. Her arms crossed up over her head, all her parts intricately carved and exposed. She too, was surrounded by candles and well lit. Jax couldn't believe his eyes. Their worst fears resided in this little bit of elephant horn. He laughed to himself, but not quietly enough. The monk that led him stopped in his tracks, turned and gave Jax that same scolding stare that the first monk had.

Jax stopped in his tracks. He threw his arms up to avoid the ass whooping that this little kid looked like he could easily dish out. He was obviously no match for Jax, but he needed to keep his cover. The kid growled and turned back toward the sanctuary. As they approached the stage. Jax realized just how big the portrait was, and standing at the edge of the stage, realized that the man in the painting was pointing toward the statue, not toward the people that gathered there. "Nice touch." Jax was really impressed with the lengths this guy went to convince his flock.

The monk told Jax to wait there, that Josiah would meet him here shortly, and turned and walked back the way they had come. Jax nodded and continued to look around the room. He walked around the stage and found a set of steps up onto the platform. He went up and stood under the painting first. He had a penchant and an eye for art at one time. This one was not done by hand. It looked like the paint had been applied by a machine. The strokes were uniform, as was the thickness of the paint. "What kind of madness is this? Who painted this?" He turned and found he was the only one in the room still. He shrugged and turned his attention to the statue behind him.

It was surrounded by candles. The heat they gave off surprised him. They were carefully placed around the pedestal that the statue was placed on. The statue itself was not much to look at. Just a long and slender woman's body carved into ivory. Larger than it looked from a distance, but still tiny in comparison to its surroundings. He stretched his arm between a gap in the candles to touch the statue. He yanked his arm back and caught his sleeve on fire as he yanked his arm away from the statue.

A man cleared his throat from the back of the room. Jax blew at the flames on his cloak and patted until the flames were extinguished. He turned to face the man in the painting as he approached the stage. "I was just wondering. That's a beautiful statue. Who is that?"

"That is The Lady Sophia. Carved from ivory in the early 14th century."

"So, we worship an old lady here?"

"No. We worship Dongorul. The Lady Sophia was a sacrifice to Dongorul. The first in written history. Have you not heard the stories?"

"Can't say that I have. That's interesting." Jax thought it was very interesting and for the first time, had a glimpse into how Beverly chose her prisons.

"What's interesting?"

Jax contemplated his answer. He couldn't say that the fact that Dongorul was trapped inside a carving of his first documented sacrifice was interesting. He was here to gather information. Not give it away. He made something up. (Make something up!)

Jax couldn't wrap his head around why they would worship this statue at all. Nothing in the brochure or the little book mentioned her. He knew that Josiah had to know that Dongorul was trapped inside it. Did he let his followers in on the secret too, or was there something else? "So, if we don't worship the old lady, who?"

"Donatus. The Savior of Souls."

Jax stifled a snicker. This guy was crazy. "The Savior of Souls. Really? Like Jesus or something?"

"Not exactly, no. What are you doing here?" Josiah started to walk in a circle around Jax. He knew right away that Jax was not what he claimed to be. He looked him over suspiciously.

"I came to be forgiven and..."

Josiah cut him off. "You are a demon. You do not deserve or seek redemption. Why did you come here?"

Jax was taken aback. Josiah was obviously not a human either. No human could look at his physical form and know right off that he was a demon. "What do you mean I'm a demon? I a man, just like you. Come to seek redemption. Nothing more."

"Liar! You are a demon and I demand you tell me who you are and what you are doing here." His words were forceful and demanding, but powerless. Without Jax's name, this being would have no power over him.

Jax carried on the charade. "Strong words. I am Nicholas, Nick to my friends. I came here, like all the rest of your followers, to be saved. What makes you think I'm a demon? Is this how you treat all your noobs?"

"Do not attempt to deceive me demon. I can smell the Phareli magic rolling off you. Why are you here?"

'Shit!' The gig was up. He was caught. There was no way to pretend to be human anymore. He was glad and panicked at the same time. He had to think fast. "Ok. You have me. I am a demon and I came here to convince you to worship me, instead of Dongorul. What would it take for you to...switch sides?"

"Liar! I can detect deception."

"No, you can't. If you could you would know that is exactly what I wanted to talk to you about. I have been watching and reading and I like what I see, and I want a following like this "statue" has. I'm real. I'm reachable. Wouldn't you rather follow something significant?"

"How dare you claim the great Dongorul insignificant? He is the Savior of Souls. He is the only one that can save us. What are you about?"

Jax had to be careful here. He couldn't give his real name away. The power of his name in this guy's hands would be deadly for him. He had to think quickly. He had already given his name as Nicholas. He would use Nicor's identity. That would work. "I am the demon of water. Does that quench your curiosity and quell your doubt?"

It worked. Josiah cocked his head and looked Jax over again. "You are Nicor? The demon of water?"

"Don't say it too loudly." Jax ducked his head like someone might throw something at him. "We can't have the masses using it, now."

Josiah nodded his head and contemplated the offer.

CHAPTER 29

Albert's phone rang in his pocket. He pulled it out when he stepped out of his truck. He looked at the screen. It was Beverly. Albert slid his finger sideways across the screen a couple of times and then put the phone to his ear.

"I haven't even made it in the house yet, are you serious." he said jokingly.

There was no friendly hello or a sarcastic response on the other end of the line. Albert heard crashes and bangs and male voices yelling. He stood there, listening. He looked at the phone screen again. It was Beverly's number.

He put the phone back up to his ear. He listened carefully to the voices trying to make out what they were saying. From the sound of it Beverly had pocket dialed him. He was going to hang up, but his gut told him to stay on the line.

He kept the phone to his ear as he unlocked the front door and stepped inside. He didn't want to jump in his truck and head back to the gallery in a panic if she was just having a couple of guys come in and move things around. He waited for something to tell him that wasn't what this was.

He put the phone on speaker and set it down on the table beside the recliner and sat down. He leaned back and tried to close his eyes for a few minutes. His head was starting to pound and he just wanted to rest a few minutes.

He bolted upright in the chair suddenly when he heard a female scream through the phone. His line was still connected, and he was listening as Beverly screamed something repeatedly between bangs and clangs. He picked up the phone, turned it off speaker, and listened carefully. 'She said we'll know' blew through his mind.

Suddenly, he heard Beverly's voice, at a distance and moving away from the phone. All he could make out from her yell was "taking me" and "sacrifice".

Albert hung up his phone and dropped his phone in his pocket. He grabbed his little bat from beside the recliner and his keys off the table by the door as he headed out. He jumped into his truck and drove as fast as he could back to the mine.

CHAPTER 30

Albert throws the truck in park outside the metal fence supposed to secure the mine. He gets out of the truck and walks over to it. He gives it a good shake. There's a chain holding it with a padlock on it.

The ground beneath his feet begins to tremble. Almost strongly enough to drop Albert to his knees. "Shit! It's already started."

He bolts back to his truck and slams the door. He pats on the dash. "Sorry for what I'm about to do old buddy. Saving the world calls for it."

He slams the truck into drive and bulldozes through the gate. He speeds up to the entrance of the mine and parks. He gets out and runs into the mine. He takes the long corridor down under ground. He pulls his zippo out of his pocked to light his way.

When he comes to a large open cavern, his eyes bounce around in his head trying to take in everything happening in the room. It's absolute chaos. A massive creature is in the middle of the room, grabbing up monks that are sanding in a half circle that files into a single in front of it. It's picking them up and swallowing them whole.

A body is lying on the slab just behind the massive creature. He can't see the face, but it's dressed like Beverly was the last time he saw her. She isn't moving. "Shit."

Jax is tied to a cross in the corner to the right of the slab Beverly is laying on. He's a bloody mess and is hurling curses like a madman. Promising to kill each and everyone one of them if Beverly is dead.

Albert closes his zippo and slips it into his pocket. He rushes to Jax's side and starts to untie him. "What happened to Beverly? Is she alive."?

"They'd all better fucking hope so. That piece of shit Josiah used her blood to perform the ritual before the moon was even up!"

"Where's he at now?"

"He was the first one Dongorul ate."

"Fitting I suppose." Albert looked around again. A monk came running at him out of nowhere and hit him in the arm. Albert turned around and looked at the person that hit him. It was just a kid. He couldn't have been more than eight or ten years old. Albert nodded at the kid, hopping he would understand that he didn't want to hurt him, but would if he had to.

The kid didn't take the warning. He lunged at Albert again. Jax jumped in front of Albert and grabbed the kid by the top of the head. "There is no one in this room that isn't going to try to kill you. Watch your back and go get Beverly out of here."

Before Albert could get another word out Jax and the kid were gone. Albert shrugs, recalling that Beverly said he was immortal. Jax would be alright. He turned and headed to where Beverly was laying on the slab. From his position now, he could see that it was her laying there, passed out and bleeding. It was a lot of blood.

He rushes a few steps and is confronted by two monks. He looks at their faces and sees fear. They are just kids too. Maybe teenagers but haven't hit puberty yet. He fights them off, trying not to kill them. The looks on their faces tell him they just want to feed him to Dongorul to prevent their own demise. He grabs them by their shirts and knocks their heads together and drops them. They slump to the ground, alive but not moving.

Albert can only hope they stay that way until after they get Dongorul contained. He closes his eyes for a moment, to make the wish. Instead, he gets a vision. The room starts to shake and wobble like it did when he was wearing the necklace and things come at him.

The rest of the world froze. This vision was much different. He didn't see the fight unfold. Instead, he sees Beverly die, and Jax fade into oblivion when her spell on him breaks. He is more determined than ever that he must save his friends, and the only way to do that is to stop Dongorul. He must get to Beverly, and she must be alive.

Albert snaps out of the vision and curses. "Oh, hell no! He looks toward the mass of monks and the demons in the middle of the room. Monks are flying in every direction. Jax is in the middle of the mass, tossing them this way and that.

CHAPTER 31

Albert rushes to Beverly's side. He must know how to stop this demon that is about to consume the world. He shakes her gently. She is limp but breathing. He shakes her a little harder. Still no response. He leans over her and starts to pound on her chest. He doesn't know cpr, except for what he has seen in the movies. He presses hard on her chest.

The pain in Beverly's chest in immense. She opens her eyes and finds Albert pressing hard on her abdomen repeatedly. "Stop it! I'll be ok. I just need to rest." She yells as she punches at Albert.

Albert sees her eyes open and stops pressing on her chest. "Oh good. Are you alright?"

"I won't be if you break a rib and it punctures a lung. Jesus man." She tries to sit up. "I just need time to heal. If you're considering being a paramedic, don't. You're technique sucks." Beverly tried to laugh but the pain from the slice through her neck and bruising she no doubt has now from Albert's poor life saving techniques made it come out as a wince instead. "What happened?"

She sits up and looks around Albert to the chaos of the two demons slinging monks around the room and the walls crumbling all around them. The room starts to spin. "Too soon." She says and lays back down and focuses on Albert's face.

"Well, you let yourself get kidnapped and they brought you here to be sacrificed, apparently. Jax was tied to a cross, but I cut him loose and now he's fighting monks on his way to Dongorul. I don't know what his plan is exactly when he gets there, but I don't think it's going to be pretty. We need to stop this Dongorul before he gets out. He's gonna run out of monks soon at this rate. Any ideas?"

She takes a deep breath and grabs Albert by the shirt. She pulls him close to her and whispers something to him. He listens attentively and when he understands, he repeats the whisper back to her. She nods and passes out again. He turns and storms through the cave. Beating off a group of monks along the way. When he reaches the demon, he yells his name.

"Dongorul. We should talk."

The demon halts his monk munching for a moment and turns to look at Albert. "You have no power over me, mortal." He turns his back to Albert proper, grabs another monk and swallows him whole.

Albert turns to look at Beverly and tell her he tried but it didn't work. She was lying there in a slump, breathing, but barely. He recalled how she spoke to Jax yesterday and how Jax responded when she said his whole name. The authority she commanded. He mustered his own.

Dongorul le'Ferat hear me. I command you to come to me, now!"

The demon turns and faces him, a look of shock on its

face. I rush toward Albert, gnashing its teeth and flaring what Albert believed were its nostrils, on the side of its head.

Albert starts to panic and jams his hand into his pocket. He fumbles around in his pocket and pulls out his zippo lighter. He begins to chant the words that Beverly whispered to him.

"Solnus exapting pelubus ren. Solnus exapting pelubus ren. Solnus exapting pelubus ren."

His denial of any of this stuff changed as he repeated the chant, repeatedly, louder and louder with each repeat. The demon storming toward him at break neck speed.

Beverly sits up and begins to chant along. She is bleeding heavily and dizzy but knows that Albert needs all the energy he can for the spell to work. She stares hard at Jax until he makes eye contact with her. He sees her chanting and nodding. He sees the pleading look on her face and as she chants the words.

"Solnus exapting pelubus ren." Jax begins to chant as well. Like Albert, louder and louder with each repeat.

A bright beam of light begins to spread from the center of Albert's lighter. He knows that he must concentrate. He continues to chant, louder and louder. As he does, the beam of light grows and begins to spread through the room. The demon, seeing the light, slows down his approach.

As the light reaches its brightest point, Dongorul stops dead in his tracks and turns to run the other way. He is slowly dragged back toward Albert but an unseen force. A loud buzz fills the room, a flash of light like a lightning bolt and loud crack echo in the room. Suddenly, the bright light and the demon disappear.

Albert brings his lighter up to eye level and then looks around the room. Dongorul is gone. He exhales a long hard breath. He looks over at Jax, still fighting with the monks.

"These monks are relentless. Their leader and their god are both gone but they are still fighting. What the hell?" Albert rushes off into the crowd to help Jax with the battle before Beverly can stop him.

Beverly watches from the platform for a few minutes. She laughs out loud as Jax belts out a battle cry. He looks like he hasn't had this much fun in years. There are bodies flying everywhere. Jax is ripping people apart and pounding them into the ground.

Beverly looks around the room for Albert and watches as Albert hears the battle cry from behind him and turns to see what is happening. He sees bodies, in whole and in pieces, flying in every direction.

"Ahhhhwwoooooo!" Albert returns the call to Jax.

He turns back around and receives a hard punch to the face, and another in his kidney. He falls to the ground. There are arms and legs pummeling him from all directions. He rolls into a ball to protect himself. He looks up and sees Jax steaming toward him throwing hooded figures out of his way. Another blow to the head and darkness slips over him.

CHAPTER 32

Albert opens his eyes, slowly. There is a light above him and it's blinding. He shields his eyes and looks around. He is in a hospital bed. His ribs are taped, his left arm is in a cast, and there is a tube in his nose. He pats himself down and shrugs.

He's alive. He takes a deep breath and leans his head back. He tries to recall what happened. He exhales a sigh of sadness. The last he remembered, Beverly was going to die, and Jax was going to go away forever. Water filled his eyes and a tear rolled down his cheek.

Suddenly, the door to his hospital room burst open and Jax stepped into the room. He looked up at Albert and smiled a huge smile. He rushed to Albert's side without saying a word. He looked him over before he spoke.

"Good to see you moving again man. That was close." Jax said.

Albert stared at Jax in disbelief. "What? How? How are you still...you?" He asked Jax. If Beverly had died, he shouldn't be. The door opened again. Slowly, Beverly appeared in the door way. "I'm not your pack mule Jax. What makes you think he is going to recover enough to need all of this..."

Albert started to clap his hands but was stopped by the cast on his arm. He winced and held them up to reach for her. She ran to him and gave him a big hug. She really was fine. He held her for a long time. Tears streamed down his face. He was just so glad that she was alive. "You're ok?"

"Yeah, I'm fine. Ribs and all." she laughed. "You are awake. This is good news." She wiped at the tears on his cheek.

He looked up at Jax. Amazed at all that he had done. He guessed it was Jax that saved him.. He had seen how powerful Jax was and it was impressive. He figured it was just a glimpse of what he was capable of, but that was enough.

He knew it was Jax that somehow managed to get both of them out of there. He opened his mouth to thank him. Jax cut him off with a wave of his hand. "Don't even. It's what you do for friends."

A few days later, Albert had healed enough to go home. Beverly drove him home. They pulled up in front of the house and Albert's truck was parked in the driveway. They all got out and walked inside. Albert settled into his recliner and Jax and Beverly stood in front of him. There was another recliner and a couch but they both chose to stand.

Albert looked them both over. "Have a seat? I'm settled in but would still like the company."

They just stood there.

Jax spoke. "Look man, I know you just got home from a really trying event and all, but..." his voice trailed off. "There is still a slight problem and we need your help again."

Albert looked at Beverly and she nodded. Albert leaned his head back against the plush cushion of his chair. It had been a terrible ordeal. He didn't want to think about it anymore.

He just wanted it to blow over and for things to get back to normal. He said as much.

"Really guys?" He held up his cast. "I haven't even healed from this one."

Beverly knelt in front of him and placed her hand on his knee. "I completely understand. This is a pressing matter though. Hear him out."

Albert sat up again and sucked in a breath. He didn't really want to deal with it. All he could do was hope that there wasn't any more talk about demons and witches. Something told him he wasn't going to get that luxury. "Okay, why the hell not, shoot! I'm all ears. What is going to destroy the world now?"

She gave him a confused look. There was no more impending danger. He had seen to that and done it brilliantly. She was proud of him and would do her very best to make sure that nothing like that happened ever again. She realized that it was her mistake for not securing the statue better than she had. She had remedied that and would make sure she secured any others that were that dangerous going forward.

"No, that's over with. The issued that we need to discuss is Jax."

Albert shot upright. He was confused. "What's wrong with Jax? You said he's immortal and he looks fine to me?" He eyed Jax as he spoke.

Jax patted Albert on the shoulder. "I am fine man. We need to know what you want to do with me now though."

Albert was still confused. "Jax has a body now. Can't he just go on being the way he is?"

Beverly explained the situation to him. "Jax has his current form because I cast a spell. A very powerful one."

Albert nodded. "I was there. I remember." He saw the energy it took first hand. He still didn't understand the problem though.

Beverly continued. "The energy it is taking to keep the spell cast is draining me. I can't maintain it much longer."

"I'm an old woman Albert. Centuries old, and my power isn't a bottomless well. If I don't cancel the spell soon, I could lose my ability to heal myself or cast anything other than a simple fireball spell. The drain will eventually lead to my death. That would just prolong the actual problem. We need to come up with an alternative for him."

Albert looked back and forth between Beverly and Jax. He understood what that meant for her, but what did he have to do with it. "What does that have to do with me?

Beverly explained some more. "When and if I die, and Jax is still bound to the necklace like he is, the spell would cancel itself and Jax would be forced back into you, or..." She paused.

Albert encouraged her to go on. "Or what?"

She continued. "I can manipulate the spell and he would be sent back to oblivion to live out eternity.

Albert had no idea what that meant. "Okay?"

Jax chimed in. "It means I become a sitting duck for all the other demon hunters that might be after me."

"A long list? " Albert asked, half kidding.

"An entire race for starters. Mine." Beverly interjected.

"So, how is him getting back into me a better alternative?

Beverly explained. "He wouldn't be hunted as long as he

was there. He would be imprisoned by the original spell. There would be no reason to hunt him.

Albert thought for a moment and recalled the conversation that he had with Jax before the grand finale with Dongorul and asked. "What happens to him when I die?"

Beverly sighed at the thought. When all this first started, she would have relished the thought of Jax being stuck inside a rotting corpse. She's since had change of heart. Albert and Jax both being stuck in Oblivion for eternity was not what she thought either of them deserved. She turned away, unable to think of it. She knew and wished like hell she didn't.

Albert had finally conceded that this shit was real. He believed it was all possible. Demons and witches and magic and all had completely turned his life on its head. He had no choice to believe now. He knew there was no going back. The thought that now, after everything that has happened, she was still cryptic and refusing to answer the questions like she had promised made him angry.

"Oh. Now you don't want to talk about it!" He yelled. "You ask me to believe you, and now that I do, you are just going to avoid answering my questions? What kind of shit is that?"

The room started to shake.

CHAPTER 33

"Shit! You think this is shit?" Beverly yelled back and then sucked in a breath to control herself.

"Calm down. It's just not easy to talk about. Neither of you deserve that, but honestly, it is the safest option. Jax was a hunted demon. As long as he is bound to something, he isn't. It's the equivalent of a bounty on someone's head. If they are in prison, they aren't hunted. You know that much."

"What you don't know is that there are technically several types of magic. For the purpose of this discussion, and to prevent your mortal little head from exploding, we will only be discussing personal and universal magic. Sound good?"

Albert calmed down a bit and the room stopped shaking. "Was I doing that? Jesus!" Albert tried to calm himself down further. "I'm sorry. Yes. That works. Go on please."

"Okay. Universal magic the universal pool of energy where all my magic comes from, but it's separate. When things are as they should be, I can cast a spell, and universal magic will support it and keep it in place. You follow me?"

"I think so."

Okay good. Personal magic is my own personal pool of magic. I can cast spells and do things with my own power outside of universal magic, but the spells I cast using my magic only last as long as I do. When I die, the spell breaks."

'Okay. I see that."

"Right now, my magic is what is binding Jax to the necklace. When he was inside you, he was held there by universal magic. So, when I die or am no longer able to maintain the spell I cast, Jax zaps back into you, unless we come up with an alternative."

"Is there an alternative?" Albert asked.

"Not one that will allow him his human form I'm afraid."

Albert sat there, trying to wrap his head around the situation. "So, in human terms, Jax is going to have to be trapped inside something else to not be hunted anymore."

"That's not right. You helped save the world. You deserve to be free. Is there, like a council or a judge, that we could talk to? I can explain all the good things you have helped me."

"Unfortunately, things don't work like that. Demons are lower place natives. When they are turned out, as he has been, there is no return, and the upper place is not an option, ever, because of his nature."

"So, what does happen to him if he goes back inside me? Does it make me an immortal?" He got a little more excited about the idea than he probably should have.

Beverly snorted. The excitement at the thought of being immortal was funny to her. She was already centuries old, and although not quite immortal, it was many more years than she wished it was going to be. Life is hard, filled with anguish, despair, hatred, and loss. Sure, there were some good and even happy times, but most of it was hard and ugly. Humans are lucky it is brief for them. It explains their morbid desire to chase it, but they were lucky.

"Unfortunately,", she stifled a chuckle, "it does not make you an immortal. That's a good thing. You don't want to live as long as we do. Especially not him." She counted herself lucky there. She could easily live to be five hundred years old, but death would finally become her. Jax would exist forever. The thought of that chilled her to the bone. She swallowed hard before continuing.

"That is why it's a tough decision. If Jax remains bound to you until I die, when you die, he will stay with you, bound to your soul, until I die."

"That's an issue because?" Albert didn't want to see Jax bound to him again. The silence inside his head was a long-awaited welcome, but he didn't want Jax being hunted either. It was a cruel sport with animals, and worse when people were hunted. He realized Jax was not a person, so to speak, but the logic expanded to this particular demon. He couldn't say the same for all of them, since Dongorul was not one he would want to see walking free.

"Because she could live to be five hundred! I would be bound inside your corpse for..." he looked at Beverly, guessing her current age. He raised an eyebrow and braced for a swing from Beverly as he continued. "...another three hundred years, on the safe side."

Beverly nodded in agreement. His estimate of her true age was nearly dead on and she was impressed with his ability to safely guess on the lower side. She was considerably older than that, but she would never tell him. "Yeah, not to mention, your souls are bound, you would be one in a sense, and demons can't get into heaven."

"So, what would happen to us, if we can't go to heaven? Would we go to hell?"

Jax laughed out loud. "Not that you would ever want to go there, no, we would not be allowed there either."

"So, what then?" Albert was confused. He only knew of three possible options. Heaven, Earth, or Hell. He often joked that he was already in hell here on earth, but that didn't really play in here.

"Nothingness."

"Nothingness? We would cease to exist then?"

"We would wish we didn't exist. It is an existence in nothing. Floating and swirling around, for the ages, in nothing."

"That doesn't sound so bad. I mean, we could be burning."

CHAPTER 34

Jax laughed out loud. The human understanding of Hell was comical to him. "Right. Burning, because that is what happens in hell. You humans and your made-up stories. There is no burning in Hell. Unless you are a witch demon hunter that treads where you don't belong. We might burn you..." He shot a look at Beverly. The look on her face told him he was about to lose the brownie points he had scored from guessing her age light. "A hot dog on the grill more than you like it, maybe, but you don't burn there. It's not hot. Quite comfortable actually."

Beverly nodded in agreement. "It was more comfortable there than I expected."

"You have been there?" Albert shot up. The idea of knowing not one, but two people from Hell was exciting.

"I'm not like you Albert. I'm a Phareli. Basically, a witch and a demon hunter, as a species if that makes it easier to understand. It's not my job, it's what I am. I can travel between the realms. There is a lot of bureaucratic bullshit to go through to do it, but..."

"Holy Shit!" Things were just getting deeper and deeper and Albert didn't know how to take it all in. His head started spinning. He leaned back in his recliner and thought, quietly, for a long time.

Beverly and Jax knew he needed some time to wrap his head around all of this. They agreed, before he woke up from the coma, that they would answer any of his questions and help him understand the way things really were, but right now, they needed an answer. Beverly was growing weaker by the minute.

Jax spoke up. "Look pal. I know this is a lot to take in right now. We kind of need an answer from you though. Beverly is growing weaker and the longer I stay...exposed...the higher the chances become that another hunter will be busting down the door to take me away."

Albert looked at Beverly more closely. She did look like she was exhausted. He hadn't noticed it before, but she was looking a lot older than she did when they got there. Things were starting to make sense to him. Magic explained a lot of it for him, for the moment. Beverly was using magic to keep Jax in his current form and if it was weakening her, he needed to end it for her. He absolutely did not want Jax back inside him though, whatever the cost, and he believed that Jax felt the same way. "What are the other options? I mean Jax needs to be bound, to something, not specifically me, right?"

Beverly and Jax looked at each other and then back at Albert. A panic spread over Jax's face. Binding to something meant being trapped inside an object for eternity. It would not break when Beverly died, releasing him to go back to Hell. Just trapped inside an object, forever. He hated the thought. Neither of them had an answer forth coming. They expected that the explanation of what would happen to Jax if he didn't agree to take him back would motivate him to just go ahead and say yes and they could get on with it.

Albert looked back and forth between the two of them. "Look. I spent 32 years believing that I was crazy. I don't want to be a jerk here, but the silence inside my head is amazing. I really don't want to just put it right back in there and I highly doubt that he wants to be stuck back inside either. There has to be a way to do it so it's not inside me." Albert stared hard at the necklace around Jax's neck. Then a thought occurred to him. "Does bound absolutely mean inside?"

Jax's face drooped. He had been thinking of maybe it being an option, as soon as he found himself standing before them in the flesh, but it had been a pipe dream. There was no way the magic would go for that. Demons were bound to things to imprison them. Then there was the whole being a human, with flesh, and feelings, and such.

Beverly opened her mouth to speak but a pounding on Albert's front door cut her off. No one moves. Suddenly, the door bursts open and Kovach rushes in. He stops in the middle of the room. There is something in his hands, wrapped in a soft blanket. It's tiny and moving.

He looks back and forth between Beverly and Albert. He looks nothing like the cop that stared Albert down in the interrogation room just a few days ago. Quite the opposite. His hair is greasy and pressed against his head, except for the piece that is dangling in his face. His clothes are dingy and wrinkled. His eyes are sunken in and he looks like he hasn't slept in days.

"I need your help. Her name is Analisa and I need you to

hide her and keep her safe." He hands the wiggling bundle to Beverly. "I have to go. Please. Protect her better than I could."

Kovach left just as quickly as he came. Jax followed him out the door and watched him get into a car and speed away.

CHAPTER 35

Beverly, Jax, and Albert all sat on the beach, staring out at the darkness. Listening to the waves crash on the shore. A gentle breeze blew off the waves and washed over them. Albert broke the silence among them.

"It's so strange how all this magic stuff is all tied together. I can't believe the ritual worked. Do you really think the universal magic will hold it in place forever?" Albert asked Beverly.

"It already is. I recanted all my spells when we performed the ritual and have no ties to what is happening with Jax now. I don't know why the ritual worked, but, Analisa is hidden and safe like Kovach asked and here Jax sits, in the flesh. It's boggling my mind." Beverly replied.

Jax jumped to his feet suddenly. "Something is missing! Shit, something big is missing!" He turned to Albert. "We have to go find it."

Albert turned and looked at Jax. "Can't we just enjoy the night here on the beach Jax? What could possibly be missing that would make me want to jump up and go find it?"

"Kovach!" Jax looked Albert directly in the eye with all the seriousness he could muster.

To Be Continued...

THE SEARCH FOR KOVACH COMING SOON!

The Search for Kovach coming soon!!!

An excerpt-

"Hey. Wake up. We've got company."

Jax stirs. "What do you mean?"

"Someone just broke the window in the bedroom across the hall. They haven't made it out of the room yet, but it won't be long."

Jax nodded and stood up. They crept out of the bedroom and closed the door behind them. Albert is met with a pipe to the face as he turns around.

As he crumples to the ground, Jax lunges forward and growls at the guy holding the pipe. They tumble down the stairs. Albert watches them tumble assholes over elbows and land on the bottom floor with a thud.

Albert looks up just in time to see another guy coming toward him. He sees this one early enough to jump to his feet and swing a punch at him that knocked the guy off his feet and sent him rolling backward down the stairs. He landed on top of the other guy just as Jax scooted out of the way. Jax jumped to his feet and kicked both of the guys while they were down. He looked up at Albert.

Albert put his finger to his mouth and gestured for Jax to be quiet. Albert crouched and waited. After a long moment, another guy came out of the bedroom. Albert bear hugged him and held him tight as he walked down the stairs.

Jax yanked the other two up by their arms and they went into the living room. Jax shoved the first two down on the couch and Albert dropped the third in the recliner. Albert and Jax exchanged glances and looked at the strangers sitting there in masks.

Albert spoke first. "Time to start talking boys. Who are you and what are you doing here?"

Jax crossed his arms and waited for one of them to answer. They all three just sat there. No one said anything. Jax leaned forward and met the guy in front of him eye to eye. He let out a low growl and his eyes turned black. His face morphed and twisted. "You will speak. or I will eat your heart while you watch."

The guy shook but said nothing.

FOLLOW THE AUTHOR

You can follow Christy Mann the author on the Christy Mann Author page here.

www.christymannauthor.com

https://www.facebook.com/christylynm

Find new authors and great works of fiction and non-fiction to read at

www.twistedsoulspress.com

https://www.facebook.com/twistedsoulspress

ABOUT THE AUTHOR

Author, Entrepreneur, and Advocate for Aspiring Writers

Having realized her lifelong aspiration of becoming a published author, Christy Mann's ambition extends beyond personal success. The visionary founder of Twisted Souls Press LLC and Metaphysical Times LLC, she is dedicated to nurturing the dreams of fellow writers. Through these platforms, she guides aspiring authors on their journey to create, publish, and effectively market their literary endeavors to a global audience.

Christy's stories are a tapestry of her diverse experiences and unyielding spirit. "Terrible Friend," in particular, exemplifies her keen exploration of friendship, trust, and the spectrum of human emotions, resonating profoundly with readers of all backgrounds.

In a world that values authenticity and empowers creativity, Christy Mann shines as an inspiring figure. Her literary accomplishments and entrepreneurial ventures stand as a testament to the power of determination, reinvention, and the relentless pursuit of dreams, no matter the life stage.

Connect with Christy Mann and explore her literary and entrepreneurial ventures by visiting christymannauthor.com, twistedsoulspress.com, and metaphysical-times.com.

www.ingramcontent.com/pod-product-compliance
Lightning Source LLC
Chambersburg PA
CBHW020516120726
47904CB00003B/856
* 9 7 8 0 6 4 5 7 3 8 6 1 2 *